The world had been a quiet place for centuries. Quiet because it was absolutely controlled. A new society, all female, reproducing by parthenogenesis, had mastered eugenics at the same time that it had achieved the technical ability not only to control population, but to create certain types—and certainly to feed, clothe and take care of every individual produced—from the testtubes.

For childbirth was a thing of the ancient past. As were the cruder forms of sex.

But in the State laboratories, skilled scientists continued to experiment with the few remaining male gametes and finally Cordelia, more skilled than the others, or perhaps more unlucky, achieved a male embryo which lived.

The State recognized at once that this represented an enormous threat to the society that had been so carefully nurtured.

And ordered the embryo destroyed . . .

Also by Charles Eric Maine

B.E.A.S.T.

FIRE PAST THE FUTURE

THE TIDE WENT OUT

HIGH VACUUM

Published by Ballantine Books

ALPH

Charles Eric Maine

BALLANTINE BOOKS • NEW YORK
An Intext Publisher

SBN 345-02904-6-125

Book Club Edition: July, 1972
First Printing: November, 1972

Printed in Canada.

Cover art by Dean Ellis

BALLANTINE BOOKS, INC.
101 Fifth Avenue, New York, N.Y. 10003

ALPH

Chapter One

On his hundred and seventieth birthday Old Gavor was presented with a massive birthday cake bearing one hundred and seventy electronic candles. The candles were so triggered that, at the slightest puff of breath from Gavor's dry lips, they extinguished themselves automatically and in precise sequence, spelling out in dark ephemeral lines the words *Happy Birthday*. It was an unusual touch of sentiment in a world that had long abandoned any pretension to sentiment. It was a device designed to keep the last man in a childishly contented frame of mind, and Old Gavor knew it, but he didn't care any more.

For most of the day he amused himself by blowing out the electronic candles over and over again, and the novelty remained fresh with him until late in the evening. Then he began to tire, and with the fatigue came peevishness. He took a knife and attempted to cut the cake in half, but it was made from a polystyrene compound and was quite inedible. Presently, frustrated and annoyed, he swept the thing from the table onto the luxuriously carpeted floor, where it flashed and sparked and sputtered for several seconds, then emitted blue smoke as it lay dead and mutilated.

Sulkily he crossed to the locked door and pressed the fourth button down on the adjacent control panel.

A green light winked merrily. He scowled, then went back to the remains of the polystyrene cake on the floor and kicked it viciously. It flashed, belched more smoke, then became inanimate.

A moment later the door slid open and a young woman entered. Her face was smooth and beautiful, with dark hair and olive complexion, and her brown eyes blended sincerity with a hint of the sardonic. Her translucent green dress was very brief, and her legs (which were the principal focus of Old Gavor's glazed eyes) were long and curved and pink.

She glanced at the damaged polystyrene cake and then at the old man. She shook her head sorrowfully, though there was a glint of humor in her eyes. "You're a naughty boy, Gavor," she said in a tone of mild reproof. "You could be reprimanded for this."

She picked up the cake and put it back on the table.

"I'm fed up," Old Gavor complained in his reedy voice. "All you give me are toys to play with. I'm tired of toys. I want to get around and see the world—to mix with real people."

The girl smiled. "The world is a big place and it is full of females. You wouldn't be safe."

Old Gavor snorted. "I have been a prisoner in this building for more than a generation. Maybe longer. I can't remember any more. I want freedom—I want my rights."

"You haven't any rights," the girl said pleasantly. "You are State property and we have to take good care of you."

"I can take care of myself. I want to get out and walk in the towns and the open country before I die."

"You can see them all on tridim."

"Damn tridim! Damn you all! I'd rather die. I *want* to die. Tell your Mistress *that!*"

The girl took his arm and eased him gently into a chair. "Now you are being antisocial. You must remember your duty towards society. After all, you are the last man, and once you are dead we shall no longer have a source of male gametes for our laboratory experiments."

"I'm a guinea pig—that's what I am."

"Not at all, Gavor. Rather, let us say, you are a biological culture from which we can extract certain unique microorganisms that may help to save the human race."

Old Gavor spat angrily on the floor. "I don't want to be a culture. I want to be a person, to do what I want to do, to see things and people."

"There are no people any more, only women. And don't spit—it's unhygienic."

Old Gavor growled in his beard. The beard was shaggy and unkempt, covering his face like a miniature undergrowth through which his long shiny nose and restless blue eyes peeped almost apologetically. Despite his age he was spritely enough, but his spriteliness possessed a brittle enfeebled quality which was reflected in the bony structure of his skeletal hands. He was conventionally dressed in a suit of dark grey, shiny at the seat and elbows. New clothes were available to him at the snap of his fingers, but he stubbornly preferred the musty comfort of those he had worn for years.

"You're like an old horse set to graze in the twilight of its life," the girl explained. "You've had your day—and your fun."

The old man chuckled abruptly. "How many did I have? Ten thousand, twenty thousand . . .?"

"More. Nearly thirty thousand children in all, including those produced in incubators. And every one a girl."

"Not bad, eh? And I'm not finished yet."

"By no means. The incubators are still breeding your progeny. Who knows?— One might be a boy. That would change the course of history."

"I wasn't thinking of incubators," said Gavor, scowling. "I meant like in the old days. Why don't I have women to stay with me now?"

The girl smiled. "At a hundred and seventy? Besides, it's wasteful. We have more efficient methods."

Old Gavor grunted in disgust. "Glass tubes and machinery. I hate it. Besides, I'm not as old as I look. Once in a while I'd like to . . ."

"I'll speak to the Mistress about it—but it's not quite as simple as you think. There have been fundamental changes in human society during the past generations. None of the mature women of today have any personal memories of men at all, and they accept the world of women as normal. Women are born into a matriarchy and, if anything, they look upon men as obsolete freaks of nature."

"Bah!" Gavor breathed indignantly. "You send them in to me. I'll show them who's a freak."

"It's a question of basic psychology and adaptation syndromes. When you have women living together without men, there has to be some kind of emotional outlet that is independent of the male sex. In other words, Gavor, the society you are living in has become totally homosexual by sheer necessity."

"Bah!" Gavor repeated.

"The truth is that there are very few women alive today who would not be repelled by the thought of having relations with a man—with you, for instance. And those who are old enough to remember and preserve something of their former heterosexual mentality are at least fifty to sixty years passed the climacteric. They are not eager."

"What about you? You're a likely looking girl."

"I am as the others—a Lesbian."

"You ought to be ashamed to admit it."

"Shame died a natural death when Sterilin was invented. We have to adapt ourselves to the new conditions of living as best we can."

"Well, Lesbian or not, you could do an old man a good turn."

Her smile was frosty. "I should be exceeding my terms of reference. The best I can do for you is to prescribe a bromide."

"To hell with your bromide." He stood up suddenly and grasped her arms with hard bony fingers. "You're supposed to look after me and give me what I want. . . ."

She twisted her arms from his senile grip with a little flexing movement. "Don't be an old fool, Gavor. You're trying to live in a past that died a long time ago. I'm a tolerant woman, but not *that* tolerant."

She pushed him back into his chair. "Sit down and cool off. You should be making your plans for the next world instead of getting intoxicated on your gonadotropic hormones. Women are different today, and the sooner you realize it the better. They think differently and behave differently. The basic things of life are different. Men are no longer necessary, and women don't miss them."

Old Gavor attempted to sneer, but his beard concealed the twist of his lips. "How about the next generation? Incubators won't help you there."

"We don't use incubators, other than for experimental work in embryology. The next generation is assured. Our scientists discovered the secret of induced parthenogenesis many years ago. We can produce the next and every subsequent generation to order, by means of drugs and radiation."

"It's not natural. . . ."

"We don't rely on nature any more. Science is more reliable. Parthenogenesis works and will go on working throughout eternity."

"But only girls—never boys."

"Of course. That's the beauty of it—the simple basic economy. Parthenogenesis can only produce females, and those females can only produce more females.

There will never again be another natural male birth unless we can create a male embryo artificially in the laboratory, and that seems unlikely."

"I don't like your world," Old Gavor said sadly. "It is cold and inhuman. All those women having drugs and radiation, without love, without any kind of human relationships . . ."

"Stop feeling frustrated and sorry for yourself, Gavor. The women are happy enough and they love each other. You see, they don't know about the drugs and the radiation. That is a State secret. Women believe that parthenogenesis is natural, that it is a modern miracle of nature to compensate for the disappearance of man. They marvel at it. They delight in it."

"So you don't even stop at deception."

"The truth is not always politic. Society is in the process of adapting itself to new conditions of living. We in authority must do our best to help the adaptation along, with the consultant advice of our giant computer systems. A white lie here, a little merciful distortion there, and a little general enforcement of overall long-term policy. The object is to preserve social stability."

"By encouraging Lesbianism . . . ?"

"That is only one factor among many. In a way you are privileged, Gavor. You have lived long enough to witness the birth of a new era in human affairs—the creation of a completely different society in a new kind of world. When you die, as you will soon, history will start again for a new humanity of only one sex. We are trying to plan ahead, to anticipate the social forces that will operate in the years to come—and to legislate for them in advance."

Old Gavor shook his head slowly. "You are using ideas that an old man doesn't understand. I'm tired. I don't want to hear any more."

"That's better," the girl said gently. "You've had an

exciting birthday and it's getting late. Time you thought about going to bed."

Old Gavor regarded her sulkily. "I should have thought that on my birthday, at least . . ."

"I promise that I'll mention it to the Mistress. She may be able to find a volunteer, but it may take time. Well, goodnight, Gavor."

He didn't bother to reply. She left the room quickly and the door locked itself automatically. He was only conscious of the offensive words that echoed and re-echoed in his brain: *She may be able to find a volunteer. . . ."*

If I am the last man, then I ought to be king of the world, he told himself in a mood of childish resentment. I ought to be the Patriarch, with unlimited power. But what am I really? Just an old man confined to a suite of rooms. I'm a prisoner, and I can't even be sure that I *am* the last man. I only know what they tell me, and it may be a lie. These new women have their own standards of conduct, and their ethics I don't even begin to understand.

Only a hundred and twenty years before there had been at least four thousand men in the State Male Reservation. Those were the good old days, before the parthenogenesis business came out in the open, when men were still necessary, human stallions in a stud farm, with nothing to do but keep the birth statistics from falling to zero. And all the time the women were waiting and praying for the birth of a male child, as if they expected some kind of second Messiah—but it never happened. Once nature starts something, she never lets up.

It was the Pill that did it—that long-term sterilizing tablet named Sterilin. Just one dose a year and a woman could forget about pregnancy. That was when the rot set in—the decay of moral standards, the era of penis and vagina worship. But from blind nature's point of view all that had happened was that the female sex had become progressively infertile. And, of course, nature compensated, as she always does. If females were infertile, then there was a need for more and more female births to redress the balance, and so gradually over the years more and more girls were born and fewer and. fewer boys. And by the time the governments of the world identified the trend it was too late to do anything about it. It was like a bloody great flywheel—it takes a long time to get moving and just as long to slow down, and the time scale was longer than human generations. So the male sex virtually died out because it wasn't being born.

And yet, in a way, men had only themselves to blame. They allowed themselves to be rounded up and used as a kind of fertility machine. They could have been masters of the situation. Instead they lived from day to day as impregnators, telling themselves that what they were doing was a solemn duty for the sake of a dying humanity, and gradually the women took control. The men could not see that the State Male Reservation was the first step in the establishment of a new kind of dictatorship. Nor did they know that artificially induced parthenogenesis had solved the problem of survival. For all the time, in their back rooms, the scientists, psychologists and sociologists had been at work restructuring a new society without men. The foundations were being laid while males were still, by law, required to impregnate countless thousands of females—only to produce more females.

What happened was that when parthenogenesis came it was clear that humanity could survive on a female monosexual basis, but only at the cost of drastic changes in emotional habits and behavior. Nor was a world without men in the least attractive to women—

then. So the men were rounded up, the few survivors, and kept to serve selected women, always hoping for the one male birth that could save the situation. No group in history received the care and attention that these last men on earth were given. They became an isolated unit cut off from the world outside, and eventually the only world they knew was the routine of sex demanded by legislation—and in time that gave way to automated methods of collecting sperm by means of machines. And always the necessity to maintain health, longevity—and isolation.

But all the rest of the world knew was that men had finally disappeared and become extinct. Adaptation was top priority. The parthenogenetic age had finally arrived, and could go ahead as planned.

And when, after many years—indeed, generations—some of the remaining men grew restless and began to demand their liberty, they were split up, dispersed throughout the world, each man assigned to work in conjunction with a particular laboratory to aid in the desperate search for a living male embryo. That was the last Old Gavor ever saw of any man. And that was many, many years gone.

He muttered pettishly to himself in the way of a very old man. Yet his thoughts were clear. He thought: they may all be dead, or some may still live. They tell me that I am the last man, but perhaps they tell the others the same. Why? To make us feel privileged? To make us feel helpless? To make us feel that nothing we may do can matter anymore?

Even the natural sexual functions are denied, and have been for years. Science has replaced the concubine with the injection, the light anesthetic, the glass tubes and the glittering equipment. They take what they want, and in return they provide shelter, food, and electronic toys like three-dimensional color television and polystyrene cakes with automatic winking candles.

What is going on in the world outside? What are the women doing with the complex civilization that men created? They give me hints and broad outlines, but how much of it is true? How much of what I see on television is live?—Or is it all prerecorded indoctrination? Their big ethical thing about selective science, for instance—the canalizing of research into functional economic projects. No more unprofitable ventures into ultrasonic flight or rockets into space. The world itself is waiting to be developed, and the sciences must be applied in the service of humanity and the State. Science is no longer the pursuit of knowledge for its own sake; it has become an instrument of the State, designed by the State to improve and strengthen the machinery of the State. One more step towards the human anthill, perhaps.

They tell me I'm a hundred and seventy today. Who the hell knows? I don't feel a day over sixty. Still, I'm an old man, there's no doubt of that. There can't be long to go for me, and I've nothing to lose anymore. Just to look around—that's all I ask. To break loose for a while and be free, and to have friends. I keep asking, but they give evasive answers.

Hell, I've nothing to lose if I force the issue. They can't kill me while I can still produce what they want for their incubators and test tubes. And even if they do, well, death isn't very far away in any case.

I'll do it. Tonight. Now.

Chapter Two

Exactly what it was he intended to do, Old Gavor would have been hard put to define. There was an urgency in his mind that had to be relieved on a tactical basis, for there was no way of thinking ahead. He knew virtually nothing of the vast building in which he had lived for more years than he cared to remember. His entire world consisted of four air-conditioned, thermostatically-heated rooms, comfortably furnished, with the usual toilet accessories, plus an exercise room with skillful built-in massage units and an artificial sun. He had never explored beyond the heavy roller door at the end of the corridor—nor did he know whether his apartment was above or below ground level, for there were no windows to guide him.

Escape, in the first instance, was a simple matter of getting beyond the roller door. It was always locked, and was opened only when one of the female attendants entered or left the apartment, either at his summons or, unsummoned, to bring him food or drink. The door, which seemed to be electrically operated, would roll back, remain stationary for about four seconds, then quickly close again. That was his only avenue of escape.

His mind pecked sluggishly at the problem in a superficial bird-like way. Ordinarily there could be no chance of his rushing the door while it was briefly open; the women assigned to attend to him were strong and well versed in the art of self-defense. It seemed to him that the solution to the problem would have to be a violent one, and he was now somewhat frail for violence, even against a woman.

He picked up a chair, weighing it speculatively in his hands. The thing was made of metal tubing and flexible plastic. It was light, easy to swing, but hard enough to serve as a weapon. He carried the chair down the short corridor to the roller door, then pressed a wall button. The green light flashed. Immediately he returned to the roller door and picked up the chair, holding it above his head, hands tightly clenched on the rigid tubing of the backrest.

A brief eternity seemed to pass before the door began to move. Old Gavor found his body trembling with excitement. He took a deep breath and waited. In a moment the door was open and the beautiful olive-skinned girl was looking at him with startled eyes. He hesitated no longer. The chair swung downward with all the force his feeble muscles could exert. The sound of the blow was sickening. One instant the girl was standing there—next instant she was a crumpled shape on the floor.

Dropping the chair, he seized her arms and dragged her into the room. Exultation bubbled within him—the girl was unconscious, the door was open, and there was nothing to prevent his escape. Except the chair. Forgetting about it momentarily in the exertion of the moment as he pulled the girl across the floor, he walked backwards into the hard rectangular shape and fell over with a crash, his legs entangled in chrome tube and plastic.

Cursing loudly he pushed himself to his feet, holding an injured shoulder, and hurled himself towards the roller door. He was a fraction of a second too late. Within inches of the door, he was dismayed to see the gleaming wall of metal glide swiftly across the opening with scarcely a sound.

Angry and frustrated, he beat upon the cold hard surface of the door with his bare hands. There was no indentations, no cavities, no sign of a concealed key-hole—it was impregnable. Nevertheless, there had to be a way of opening it from the inside. The attendants could do it, though he had never learned how. Some electronic device, perhaps—a hidden transmitter concealed in their clothing, radiating an impulse signal at the touch of a button.

The girl was still unconscious, so there was time to find out—but not much time. Hurriedly, with trembling fingers, he patted the brief clothing she wore but could feel nothing beyond the soft shape of her body underneath. His hands began to linger a little and then he came upon the belt. It was beneath her short dress, clipped around her waist, and he could follow the shape of it with his fingers. It seemed to him to be thicker than a belt might reasonably be expected to be. On its surface he could feel the protruding discs of buttons.

In triumph he flung back the dress, exposing the lower part of her body. Apart from the belt she was unclothed, but it was the belt that demanded his immediate attention. It was of some flexible metal, blue-grey in color, and on either side of the center clip were four silver push-buttons. Excitement possessed him; he might be old, but when it came to the point he was no fool.

He struggled with the clip to release the belt, but it refused to open. Baffled for a moment, he stared at it in anger, then realized abruptly that he was wasting time. If the thing was radio activated, then all that was necessary was to press the right button and the door would open—but which button?

As he sat reflectively, making up his mind, the girl stirred. It was just a spasmodic movement of one leg, but suddenly the mechanism of the belt did not seem to matter anymore. Until she moved she had been an inert body, a waxwork, but with the movement came a sense of animation, of life, and she became a woman, already bared to the waist. Something mischievous began to jig about in his brain. Her helplessness electrified him. He stroked her legs and moved them apart, enjoying a tactile exploration that had been denied to him for many years.

He was an old man, was he? Well, he could show them just how old he was. There was plenty of life in the old skeleton yet. In fact, there was less life than he hoped for, and his response proved to be painfully slow. His sense of urgency melted into a mood of stubborn determination. I'll press the button later, he thought. There's no hurry. I can afford to wait a few minutes.

The act of rape turned out to be more difficult and less satisfying than he had imagined, and he realized that he was old, after all—very old. But he persevered in a mood of single-minded aggression, thankful for his own self-respect that she was still unconscious, and presently, having achieved his object, he felt ashamed of himself.

He pressed the silver buttons one by one. At the fifth contact the roller door opened.

You are in a corridor without windows, mellowly lit by a luminous ceiling. It curves on either side to a vanishing point, and is level. It may be high in the air or deep beneath the ground; there is no way of knowing. In one direction or the other lies escape and freedom. It may be one hundred feet away, or one thousand yards. There may be a staircase, or an elevator, or a pneumatic drop shaft, or a spiral incline. It is all in the future, and in some curious way time and space have become intermingled, for each step forward is a second in time, and the seconds and distance merge so that the two are no longer independent. You count the seconds and you count the footsteps, and behind all is the rhythm of your own heartbeat, counting off the moments to release or annihilation.

The building is deserted. You come upon a staircase leading to an upper level. So you ascend, cautiously, flexing your ankles to avoid making any sound. There is another corridor, another flight of stairs; you keep ascending. And presently there are no more stairs, and the corridor you are in is a cul-de-sac. There are doors, four of them, in the corridor, but they are of the metal roller type and there is no way of opening them. If you had had the patience and the common sense to remove the electronic belt from the olive-skinned girl you raped not so long ago, you would have been able to open the doors. Perhaps behind those doors are the other last men of the world, sealed away forever until the liberating moment of death.

No time to pause or worry about them, if indeed they exist at all. Time is running out. The olive-skinned girl might be conscious by now, or she might be missed. At any moment the alarm might be raised. Escape becomes a precision operation, a matter of split-second timing—difficult enough even when you are young.

This must be the top, for there are no more stairs and no elevators. There is nothing left but to descend, as quickly as possible on feeble trembling legs. Four flights, five, six and seven . . . and still the building is deserted. Can it be that there is only one woman in the entire structure? But no—for you yourself have seen several different faces, three or four, and there is also the Mistress in charge. In charge of what? A prison, an asylum, a clinic? How large or small a staff would be required to run such an establishment?

There is no answer to your question, and the building remains silent. Perhaps they know that escape is unlikely or even impossible. Perhaps they believe that the prisoners prefer the austere comfort of their apartment cells to what lies outside. Perhaps the outside world has become so alien that no man would voluntarily seek escape into it.

There can be no turning back. You have committed a criminal act by any code of conduct, and the need for escape becomes more pressing as each second ticks by. But where is the outside world? How can one locate it in a tall building of windowless corridors and stairs, with uniform illumination and temperature, so that each level is identical with the one above and the one below?

Descend. Quickly at first, then more slowly, for you are an old man and your energy has no depth. Level after level: steel, alloy and plastic: curving corridors and roller doors, featureless, identical, with no humanity. Perhaps you are now descending below ground level and any one door might be the exit to the outside world, but there is no way of opening it. You have exchanged one prison for another. There is no escape, and you can no longer remember the location of your own apartment—it is lost in the maze of levels and corridors and doors.

After an hour you begin to tire, so you sit on a stair to think. You recall, with a certain sense of irony, that at no time have any special precautions been taken to prevent violent escape. The female attendants, all young, have always been unarmed and vulnerable. The reason begins to permeate your weary brain: Escape is impossible. The building is a maze, a rat trap, a geometrical structure without form or orientation, always curving back upon itself. The roller doors in the corridors might well be fakes, for all you know, and perhaps there is only one apartment—the one you vacated an eternity ago—and all the rest is an elaborate facade designed to deceive you. Perhaps the building was constructed to tire the would-be escaper, to disillusion him and destroy his spirit. In an old man that is not so difficult to accomplish.

You continue to stumble down the stairs, rapidly losing faith and enthusiasm, and even regretting your desperate bid for freedom. This must be the fourteenth or fifteenth level, above or below ground you do not know, but you are still descending. It might be that as you are descending the levels are moving upwards in some kind of infernal squirrel cage, so that you will descend forevermore.

At the twentieth level you stop—there is still no exit. Escape has become an abstraction with no basis in reality. Even worse, there is no way of returning to your own comfortable apartment.

And still the stairs go down, falling endlessly into a bottomless pit, spiraling eternally into the abyss. You realize that you are a fool, an old fool. Why didn't you stay in your dull but cozy apartment, taking life as it came? Why bother to worry about the outside world when it has long since left you behind? Surely it is enough to survive and be looked after by pretty girls, even if they use machines to draw off your seed at regular intervals for their laboratory experiments.

There must be somebody in the building—the Mistress, the attendants. Without them one could wander forever up and down the stairs and along the silent corridors. One could thirst and starve to death in desolate isolation, surrounded by closed doors. There is nothing left to do but appeal for help and mercy. You shout, louder and louder, until suddenly you realize in horror that you are screaming. . . .

She comes unexpectedly, perhaps minutes, perhaps hours after you have abandoned all hope. She is the olive-skinned girl you raped a thousand years ago. Her face is a beautiful mask, and there is no feeling or emotion in her eyes, not even hatred. You push yourself unsteadily to your feet, feeling more like an animal than a human being. She stands on a higher stair, symbolically remote and on another plane of existence. Her eyes are steady and you cannot face them. . . .

"So you wanted to escape," said the girl. Her voice was calm, without rancor or accusation.

"Yes," Old Gavor sighed. "I had the idea. I thought it would be easy. I didn't realize . . ."

"There are many things you do not realize, old man. You are out of touch with reality."

He hesitated. "Death is very close to me. Right and wrong have lost their meaning. There are things I want to do. . . ."

"And things you have done."

He sensed the implication of her words, and nodded humbly. "I am sorry. . . ."

"Sorrow is meaningless. What is done is done. You sought escape and you shall have escape. It is the rightful privilege of the last man. In any event, we do not need you anymore."

"I am no longer sure that I want freedom."

"We are just. You shall have what you sought. Follow me."

She turned and ascended the stairs. He followed her mechanically, stumbling over the steps, forcing himself upwards in defiance of the paralyzing weariness that was creeping into his limbs. He felt cold and shivery, as if *rigor mortis* were already invading the fiber of his body.

Two flights, three flights, they ascended, and suddenly they were facing a roller door in a corridor. She turned to him, and for the first time he thought he could detect an element of humanity and sadness in her eyes.

"You will not be the first to pass through this door," she said, "but you will be the last. Men do not vary. Even unto death they seek to enlarge their horizons, and they always seek escape. I shall not stop you now. Escape if you wish."

Her fingers touched her waist, pressing a concealed button on the unseen belt. The door rolled silently aside. Old Gavor remained motionless.

"Go," she ordered.

He hesitated. "Tell me—am I really the last man?"

There was a ghost of a smile on her lips. "You are what you are, Gavor. Once you are dead there will be neither men nor women in your world. Now go."

Old Gavor walked into the corridor beyond the door.

The corridor was long and dark, and as he walked along it the air grew progressively colder. Old Gavor shivered in his somber grey clothes. But there was a faint glow of light on the walls ahead and he hurried toward it on his stumbling legs.

The glow became brighter and the cold more intense. Presently the corridor came to an end, and he was finally in the open air, under a sky of midnight blue with an immense crimson sun lying low on the horizon. Something flickered and undulated above him —in a brief glance he observed the intermittent luminous curtains of aurora. The air howled with wind, and the ground was white with snow and ice. His breath frosted as it left his lips.

For fully a minute he stood motionless, surveying the wasteland, aware of the biting sting of cold in his flesh and bones. The immense white wilderness before him was bleak and empty; it might have been a plateau in Antarctica, a hostile expanse of sub-zero landscape devoid of life and hope. The midnight sun glimmered dully—it was the color of blood.

He turned around toward the corridor, but it was already sealed. The gleaming width of a metal door stared blankly at him. Above and on all sides the building towered—solid, cylindrical, with no light, but reflecting the dark red glow of the polar sun from its rounded concrete surface.

Many things became clear to Old Gavor. This was the prison, a citadel in a remote frigid corner of the world. This was the last abode of man and the final sepulcher of the male sex. The freezing wind whined in his ears and plucked at his clothes, paralyzing his body with every gust. He hammered on the door and screamed against the noise of the elements, but his voice was drowned in the tumult of nature.

How many men, he wondered, have perished this way, seeking freedom? How many have sought civilization, only to find raw nature? How many frozen bodies are out there in the ice and snow, dreaming the blank dreams of death, while thousands of miles away the world they knew has reshaped itself and forgotten them and their kind?

He hammered and screamed, but the door remained closed, and in the course of time the cold became gentle and transformed itself into sleep. Acting on some deeply buried instinct he moved off into the snow, away from the building, toward the crimson sun, as if seeking privacy for the final intimate act of his life.

If I am the last man, he thought, *then this is indeed a moment of history.*

Within the hour his body was buried beneath inches of snow and the blood in his veins had crystallized into scarlet ice.

Chapter Three

Five hundred years later an event of major importance occurred in the government biological laboratory No. 5. Cordelia, the scientist in charge of experimental synthetic cytology, took the trouble to lock the incubator and secure the laboratory door before leaving the State Biophysical Center. The thing in the main thermostatically controlled incubator was so vital that she felt impelled to deliver the progress report in person to the Senior Mistress of Applied Cytology in the Ministry of Biophysical Research.

Cordelia, a handsome woman of seventy-two, had made full use of modern cosmetic techniques, and her metabolic control had been precisely judged for more that two decades. Consequently, she had all the superficial appearance of an adolescent female, except for the heavy maturity of her eyes and the overfull roundness of her breasts and abdomen—the result of three compulsory visits to State fertility centers, where induced parthenogenesis had resulted in the births, over a number of years, of identical baby girls.

But her mind was wrinkled and leathery, impregnated with specialized science and technology, and twisted in the accepted Lesbian fashion of contemporary society. The thing in the incubator was in its own way alien and incomprehensible to such a conditioned woman, but nevertheless it represented success of the highest order. For centuries women scientists had labored after the shadow, as the alchemists of ancient history had sought the Philosopher's Stone, and now, finally, the shadow had taken material shape. The thing in the incubator represented the pinnacle of scientific achievement—but it might also prove to be the problem of all time.

She traveled by autorail and underground mobile roads to the select government zone of the city, and ascended to the forty-third story of the Department of Applied Science and Technology. There was some difficulty with the receptionist and the under-secretary; the Senior Mistress of Applied Cytology was by no means readily available to casual visitors. After a twenty-minute delay she was finally admitted to the under-secretary's office, and half an hour later she graduated to secretary level. Ten minutes later she reached the inner sanctum and found herself greeting the Mistress herself.

The Mistress was a woman of indeterminate age, fleshy without being fat, rigid without being bony. Her face was flaccid, her eyes small but deep, and therefore oddly remote. Her flat bare breasts were lacquered purple, as was the custom among higher government officials. She wore a short black skirt and black sandals, contrasting with her cropped hair, which had been varnished snow white.

"Please sit down, Cordelia," said the Mistress of Applied Cytology. "I must apologize for keeping you waiting, but pressure of work is such that—well . . ." She smiled thinly. "Unexpected interviews are invariably difficult to arrange at short notice."

Cordelia nodded sympathetically. "I understand and apologize, Mistress. But I have some very important news for you about Test 454."

The Mistress opened a drawer in her desk and produced a file, which she opened, withdrawing a number of papers. She flicked through them rapidly, then selected one particular typewritten sheet.

"Test 454," she murmured thoughtfully. "That's in the sex-related chromosome-linkage series."

"The Antarctic man," Cordelia explained. "The one they found buried deep in the ice about three years ago."

"I remember."

"He died about five hundred years ago, and there is reason to believe that he may have been the last man. He was in a remarkably well preserved state. We were able to isolate many thousands of perfect cell nuclei—gametes, of course, with twenty-three chromosomes and the masculine DNA factor. The cells were dead, but the chromosomes were transferable. It took a long time to perfect the technique—precision microcytology using scalpels invisible to the naked eye. We had to remove the DNA chromosome structure from a male gamete and transfer it to a living female ovum, matching them perfectly so that natural affinity would take place, so that mytosis would occur and the cell would live, divide and grow."

"I know—I know . . ."

"Well, the gametes of the Antarctic man were shared among eighteen cytological laboratories. I had an allocation of gametes along with the rest. Four days ago I performed my four hundred and fifty-fourth microcytological transfer."

"And—what happened?"

"I succeeded, Mistress. The cell is still alive. It has already divided and subdivided more than twenty times, and each new cell has its basic forty-seven chromosomes—the masculine genetic structure. I have checked with the ultraviolet phase-contrast microscope. There is no mistake."

The Mistress of Applied Cytology pursed her lips and studied Cordelia as if she were a new virus strain.

"In other words," she said, "you claim to have produced a living male embryo."

"Exactly."

"For the first time in over five hundred years."

"Yes."

The Mistress stood up and wandered thoughtfully around the room, stroking her rectangular chin and frowning in mild perplexity. She said: "Which incubator are you using?"

"The Reissner thermostatic radiation chamber."

"I see. How long will it take for the embryo to develop beyond primary gestation—to foetal status?"

"Within present parameters, I should say less than ten weeks."

"With a positive physical determination of sex?"

"Undoubtedly."

The Mistress returned to her desk and made a note on a small pad. "Do you think it will survive—this embryo?"

"I am certain of it. The cell division is vigorous, and so far, perfect in every way."

"Who else knows about this experiment—Test 454?"

"My two assistants."

"What are their names?"

"Wistaria and Tosta. Do you want their registration numbers?"

The Mistress shook her head. "With an experiment of this kind, particularly when successful, we have to make sure that there can be no possible leakage of information. The Minstry, I think, will transfer Wistaria and Tosta almost immediately, and will also change the site of the experiment. The incubator and its associated equipment will be moved to a more secure location."

Cordelia blinked and opened her mouth as if about to speak, but said nothing. The Mistress of Applied Cytology smiled shallowly.

"This is not the first time we have had promising indications, of course. On many occasions cytologists have succeeded in creating a forty-seven chromosome embryo by microbiological and parthenogenetic techniques. The embryo would divide and grow, but only for a short time. Naturally we are most anxious to avoid the spread of rumor and false information—therefore we have to take stringent precautions."

"I understand," Cordelia murmured.

"We have a special laboratory reserved for what we define as alpha projects. What is more, we have a special staff of trained cytologists to take over such projects and develop them under carefully controlled conditions."

"You mean that I am to be relieved of my part in Test 454?"

"Not at all, Cordelia. You will work in liaison with our alpha scientists. After all, you may be able to help them in many ways, initially."

"And then . . . ?"

"If the embryo survives and grows, then the alpha scientists will probably take over completely. You see, Cordelia, the development of a live male embryo is not simply an abstract scientific experiment. There are certain important social ramifications. There have been no living males in the world for some five hundred years, and an experiment of this kind, if it succeeds, must be considered and analyzed from very many angles. Indeed, it moves from pure science into politics."

Cordelia regarded her superior thoughtfully, striving to read beyond the glassy inscrutable surface of the other woman's inscrutable eyes. There was no sense of psychic contact—never had been between people for as long as she could remember, except when the parthenogenetic adaptation syndrome produced emotional affinity that resolved itself in physical eroticism. A new and startling idea invaded her brain: *We're robots, she and I,* Cordelia thought. *We're integers in some vast impersonal social equation. We are not even individuals because we do not have the right of individ-*

ual action anymore. We are part of the mechanism, cells in the superior planetary body of integrated womankind; our mass brain is a network of electronic computers, and our conduct is controlled and predicted by computer programs on magnetic tapes.

The feeling came and went, phantom-like. The Mistress condensed into solid humanity again, and her hard fleshy face became earthy and workaday. "Return to your laboratory," she said. "Meanwhile I shall confer with the Ministry. In the course of a few hours I shall communicate with you and give you detailed instructions."

"And my assistants—what shall I tell them?"

The Mistress's lips shaped a stillborn grin. "By the time you reach your laboratory they will already have gone. You will never see them again."

The new laboratory was a subsection of the secret research center of the Ministry's Department of Applied Cytology. It was buried more than one hundred feet below the ground, directly beneath the tall skyscraper block that housed the immense staff of the Ministry of Biophysical Research. Cordelia had never even suspected the existence of the place, which was not surprising in view of the meticulous security precautions. She found that she was obliged to live underground in a small apartment adjacent to the laboratory itself; ten other research cytologists lived underground, too. For three months she worked and slept beyond sight of sky or sunlight, breathing filtered air, living in perpetual artificial illumination, working at the gleaming chrome and plastic benches or the shining cylindrical incubators, sleeping naked under the ultraviolet ceiling lights that kept her body bronzed and healthy. She worked under orders, for she was no longer a responsible scientist in her own right; she was now a member of a team, and the other cytologists were women who had been specially selected for work of high security value.

Test four-five-four was by no means the only experiment in progress. Cordelia was astonished to learn that there were as many as seventeen male embryos in the thermostatically controlled incubators of the laboratory —but one by one they died. To create a male embryo was apparently not so difficult, but to secure its survival was another matter.

Embryo four-five-four, however, did not die. "Incredible," they said, seeking an explanation. It was a matter of indefinables, of some subtlety in the precise mechanism of surgical microcytology, of some discrete factor in the transfer of DNA and RNA modules from a frozen male gamete. It was a miracle of patiently applied science that might not be repeated in a decade, or a century, or ever again.

The embryo grew and began to differentiate. Limbs began to appear, and a head and a beating heart. The artificial placenta supplied oxygenated blood to the tiny living creature, while the saline solution in which it was immersed maintained a constant temperature of ninety-eight point four degrees Fahrenheit.

Gestation was rapid, accelerated by carefully conceived electronic control. Cordelia's estimate of ten weeks proved to be too pessimistic. At the end of eight weeks the embryo was already a male child weighing four pounds, still attached to its artificial placenta but moving its limbs with aggressive energy. It became apparent that the foetus would within a few weeks be ready for independent existence—ready for severance from the placenta and removal from the saline solution. Or, as Cordelia recognized (with a faint feeling of revulsion which had its origin in compulsory fertility and parthenogenesis), ready for birth.

Her personal interest in the male child grew steadily from day to day. Sometimes she fell to speculating about the future of the child—*her* child—in the incubator. What role could one male fulfill in a monosexual society that had adapted itself to its own specialized mode of existence and survival over the centuries? Was there any point or purpose in allowing the child to survive? And supposing there were more male children—supposing the child on attaining maturity were able to reproduce his own sex in defiance of the natural inhibition that had operated for so many centuries—what then? Could human society turn the clock back and resume heterosexual living? Could women tolerate reversion to the primitive in matters of human propagation? Parthenogensis was neater, cleaner, and so precise; it was devoid of emotional contamination, and pure in that it was a function on the level of abstract duty. Impregnation by unseen radiation and untasted drugs was surely the ultimate in reproductive techniques, and no modern woman could contemplate without horror the violation of her body in crude physical fertilization by a creature that had been extinct for hundreds of years. It was unimaginable.

And yet there was something appealing about the child in the incubator, something that occasionally caught the heart, like an injection of adrenalin, and produced an indescribable writhing of the fundamental emotions. And Cordelia was conscious of a very special feeling of proprietorship, for it was she who had performed the original microcytological transfer that had injected the breath of life into the pink and wrinkled midget inside the glass tank. The child was here, as surely as if she personally had given birth to it in a State fertility center; and as the foetus grew and developed to the stage of imminent independence, she experienced something akin to pride—and, presently, to love.

On the day they removed the male child from the incubator and slapped it into lusty bawling, the Senior Mistress of Applied Cytology visited the underground laboratory. Her square jaw was firm and unsympathetic and her eyes were cold. Cordelia sensed, in subdued alarm, a certain critical quality in her attitude.

The Mistress inspected the baby but betrayed no reaction.

"Weight?" she inquired.

"Eight pounds four ounces," Cordelia announced proudly, as if she personally had given birth to a son.

The Mistress's eyes traveled the length of the tiny body in the enclosed plastic crib.

"There's no denying the maleness."

Cordelia said nothing; there was an acrid quality in her superior's voice that she did not like. Several of the other scientists had gathered round to hear the Mistress's comments. Theye were impassive in their attitude. The baby might have been a stained specimen on a microscope slide for all the human interest that was apparent in their eyes. Cordelia began to feel protective towards the infant under such objective scrunity.

"During the past few weeks," said the Mistress, "Test 454 has been discussed at high level throughout the world—a *very* high level indeed. Our executive scientists and politicians have acted in close liaison with the world administrative computer network, so you will appreciate that any decision they have reached is the result of long and careful deliberation, taking into account all the relevent factors and projecting all the variables on the basis of a long-range analytical forecast."

The Mistress paused to draw a deep breath and formulate her words. She went on: "You will understand that for a long, long time the principal object of scientific research in our world of today as been"—she waved a hand idly towards the crib—"this. What you see before you, alive and unbelievably active, is the end product of millions of experiments over hundreds of years—

secret experiments. Womankind throughout the world has adapted herself to life as we now know it, and a very stable and efficient form of society has been developed. We live, and live very well indeed, without a male sex—so much so that it is questionable whether society would be any better off if a reversion to bisexual conditions were to occur."

A murmur of agreement rippled round her audience. The Mistress was merely echoing opinions that had been inbred since birth in all of them.

"Nevertheless, it has always been the policy of the government to control every factor that might influence the structure of our society, and it has always been realized that a species without a male sex might, in some way, be lacking in some fundamental psychological component that . . . well, to put it simply, would maintain overall human sanity."

"Nonsense," said one of the cytologists, smiling. "As a race we are saner than ever before in history."

"Why," said another, echoing the smug complacency of her colleague, "we all know that the age of insanity was the age of men. Every child is taught that in the State school."

The Mistress smiled grimly. "Governmental policy is rather different from what is taught in State schools. Racial sanity is more than a question of racial behavior. It involves deep psychology on a mass basis—a racial neurosis, if you like. There are very good reasons for believing that the stable form of society in which we live today is essentially neurotic."

She scanned her audience like a radar antenna. "A neurosis can be extremely stable and produce a condition of balanced equilibrium, particularly when it is based upon a long-established perversion. That is roughly the condition of our society today."

Murmurs of doubtful assent and disguised bewilderment.

"All this is not just my personal opinion. It is fact,

and behind it is the full authority of the sociological
data bank of the world computer brain. Human society
is cast in the form of a perversion neurosis, but it works.
The perversion content is exactly balanced by a set of
artificial ethics—law, behavior, relationships, moralities
—designed to channel the perversion into useful and
productive streams of human energy. Above all, designed to make the women of the world happy."

"What is all this leading up to, Mistress?" asked
Cordelia.

The other women seemed to withdraw a little at her
temerity, but the Mistress merely made a pleasant face,
as if she had been expecting the question and regarded
it as an enthusiastic invitation to continue.

"I will come to that presently. First I wish to stress
the fundamentals of the problem confronting us. It is
both simple and complex. We have to consider a situation embracing a stable perversion neurosis in which the
operating conditions are a rigid impersonal totalitarianism of government coupled, strangely enough, with an
almost universal happiness.

"There are, of course, a few unhappy ones who have
not been able to adapt readily to the parthenogenetic
syndrome, but they are steadily being weeded out. Our
mortic laws see to that, and in due course all women
will conform to the pattern of the syndrome and will
consequently be perfectly happy and contented."

A general atmosphere of uneasiness was apparent
among the audience. Other cytologists had joined the
group, and they stood listening restlessly, avoiding the
direct gaze of the Mistress's cold eyes but attending
closely in a manner which suggested that they should
not be listening at all.

The Mistress's voice became more somber. "I am
telling you things that some of you, perhaps most of
you, have only vaguely suspected. As trusted government servants you already know far more than the rest
of womankind. You know the true secret of induced

parthenogenesis, and you understand why the government propagates the belief that parthenogenesis is of natural origin. It is all part of the syndrome—part of the mechanism that ensures a stable society. But I have hinted at a greater control, a firmer grasp on human affairs. Do not let it surprise you. Human affairs are no longer human—they are determined and predicted by the world computer brain network. The brain is always right. It is immensely wise and it never makes a mistake."

Cordelia ventured to speak again. It was the only way to relieve the anxiety that was building up in her mind. "All this is most interesting, Mistress, but what has it to do with Test 454?"

She felt ashamed of herself for referring to her baby by the official label, but the words were uttered and could not be recalled. She glanced towards the crib. The baby was awake, kicking at the air with small wrinkled legs and possibly crying, though no sound could penetrate the sealed plastic walls of the enclosure. But at least Test 454 was a reality, and there was little anyone could do about it, even the world computer brain.

"Test 454 must be destroyed," the Mistress stated flatly.

A multiple gasp quivered momentarily in the air as the audience reacted to the edict. Cordelia found herself suddenly chilled and shaking with fear an anger.

"That is the final decision of the world brain," the Mistress explained. "It was made only after many weeks of the most careful and detailed computation in the context of the sociological sciences."

Cordelia glanced hastily around the frozen circle of her colleagues and was encouraged by the dismay reflected in their facial expressions. She pointed to the baby. "This is no longer a test embryo, Mistress—it is a living independent human being. To destroy it would be murder."

"Not in law," said the Mistress smoothly. "The Department of Applied Cytology realized a long time ago that special provision would have to be made for experimental embryos undergoing development tests in laboratories. To regard such embryos as premature humans, as it were, would seriously hinder the progress of scientific research. The law was therefore amended. Today all experimental embryos of laboratory origin are regarded as expendable test material, unless application is made to the Department of Mortic Revenue for legal recognition of any particular test embryo as a human individual."

"Then let us make an application now."

"There would be no point. Mortic policy is determined by the world computer brain, and the brain has already delivered its verdict. Under no circumstances could recognition now be given to Test 454."

A profound silence blanketed the group. Only the remote ticking of the thermostats in the incubators disturbed the noiselessness. For a few moments everyone, except the Mistress, was looking at the baby.

"Beware of sentiment," said the Mistress, her voice controlled and calm. "What you see in the crib is the result of a successful experiment in surgical microcytology, but it is no more than a specimen and there is no question whatever of human status. Other embryos have had to be destroyed, and there is absolutely no difference of principle in this particular case."

The baby was unconcernedly sucking its thumb, not caring about status, principles or law. Cordelia noted the clear blue eyes, moving restlessly as if trying to make sense out of the shapes and lights and shadows beyond the transparent walls of the crib. They were intelligent human eyes.

Cordelia said: "May we know precisely why the world brain thought it necessary to destroy this—this child?"

"It is not a child—it is a test specimen," said the

Mistress sharply. "I have already warned you about the dangers of sentiment. Judgment must always be free from emotional distortion."

"And from mercy?"

"To talk of mercy in connection with a test specimen is meaningless. However, let me explain the way the verdict was determined in terms of the computer program. The problem was basically one of introducing an unknown variable factor into a balanced social equation, and we had to examine the many millions of permutations and combinations of social change that could result from the introduction of one live male into society as it now exists.

"We took into account the question of male reproduction by heterosexual practices, and even assumed for the purposes of one computation that within a certain number of generations the male sex, if it were perpetuated, might come to equal the female in numbers, as was the case centuries ago. We found that a stable heterosexual society would theoretically be possible in about five thousand years time, but during the intervening period there would be chaos. Society as we know it would disintegrate."

"But why?"

The Mistress sighed patiently. "Because of the syndrome—the perversion neurosis. It was caused by the biological elimination of men. If you confront a perversion neurotic with the cause of all the trouble and try to enforce a reversion to normal behavior, the result will almost certainly be uncontrollable hysteria—and hysteria in the mass is a terrifying thing. It would bring an end to rational thought and civilized conduct. Ultimately it would mean racial insanity and racial suicide."

"You mean," said Cordelia truculently, "that once women realized that men were returning into their lives they would rebel against this regimentation, this carefully computed soulless Lesbian society. They would laugh at the hallowed syndrome, as you call it, and tear your beautifully engineered social structure to pieces in sheer mutiny."

The Mistress spoke in an ominously quiet voice. "You know that is not true, Cordelia. It is not a question of rebellion or mutiny, for there is nothing to rebel against. Society is stable and womankind is happy. The problem is purely one of hysteria resulting from instability of the kind that would be engendered by a reintroduction of the male sex. Human behavior would be influenced by emotional rather than logical pressures. It would become unpredictable, which is a bad thing. The result would be widespread unhappiness, and that is even worse. There might be outbreaks of violence, suicide, murder—and even non-cooperation in required parthenogenetic routines. Finally, men, because of their instinctively aggressive nature, would seek power, ultimately to take over the government of the world, and we should go back to the era of wars and inhumanity to man. I am sure you would not like to see that happen."

Cordelia was unconvinced. "You're afraid that the government would be undermined—that someone might decide to wreck the world brain in the cause of freedom and independence. Well, let them wreck it! You talk of inhumanity to man—but how can a Lesbian society which is balanced on the razor edge of a perversion neurosis by means of totalitarian indoctrination be regarded as human or even civilized? Is stability so important, or even happiness? Are human beings the better for being predictable, even though they are perversion neurotics? Perhaps five thousand years of hysteria and chaos might be worthwhile if it results in a new kind of society with both males and females. Even the beasts of the field have *that* privilege!"

Cordelia suddenly became silent, alarmed and astonished by what she had said. The words had spilled themselves from her brain without conscious thought, and they did not even represent her true attitude. She was a loyal supporter of the State, a trusted government scientist, and never in her life had she voiced or entertained ideas of such a treasonable nature—nor did she even believe the words she had just uttered. Indeed, the words had tumbled out from some dark region beyond consciousness, uncontrollably, as if generated by some new irrational twist in her brain.

Hysteria, she thought, suddenly afraid. *The Mistress is right and the syndrome is real. The male child has started it already. Test 454 is insidiously affecting my judgment, injecting unreason into my thoughts, introducing an element of unpredictability into my reactions.*

She saw her silent diagnosis reflected in the hard set of the Mistress's eyes and in the restrained alarm of her colleagues. She had confirmed, by her words, everything that the Mistress had predicted, and it was now too late to retract or apologize. The inevitable would happen: She would be taken away to a psychoneural center and subjected to drug therapy and deep hypnosis to rid her mind of the distortion that had revealed itself so clearly. And in time she would be transferred to a new post in a new city. And Test 454 would be destroyed, anyway. She had risked her future for nothing.

"I think," said the Mistress, "that you had better come with me, Cordelia. Meanwhile, Test 454 is to be destroyed by government directive."

Chapter Four

After Cordelia and the Mistress had left, the cytologists in the laboratory talked among themselves. The conversation revealed multiple symptoms of shock, alarm, embarrassment and self-righteousness. Scientists one and all, they resented the destruction of an extraordinary experiment with which they had been involved for weeks, even as they decried Cordelia's emotional reaction. Only Koralin had nothing to say; she was a junior scientist, not yet thirty, of an introspective nature. She listened closely without change of expression, but did not contribute to the general discussion.

"Whoever would have imagined . . . Cordelia, of all people!"

"You never can tell. The quiet conscientious ones are often the most unreliable."

"But to behave in that *subversive* fashion . . ."

"And just after the Mistress had been talking about hysteria!"

"It illustrates the danger of specialization. Cordelia had worked for a long time on Test 454. She must have developed some kind of emotional attachment."

"Fatal! A scientist must always be objective."

"I admit it is difficult to regard Test 454 purely as a specimen, but after all, facts are facts."

"If we all started getting sentimental about every embryo in the incubators, where would we be?"

"What do you suppose will happen to her?"

"Nothing much—a little psychoneural treatment. The State is very lenient."

"D'you think there are other women like her—with that kind of aberration, I mean?"

"A few, perhaps. There is always an element of insanity in any group. Still, it might have been an interesting experiment to see men return to society."

"We might as well humanize apes and gorillas."

"Come, now! That in itself is an over-emotional reaction!"

"I don't think anyone would really want to revert to such times. They say men used to rule the world, and women were virtually slaves. Men used to use them as they wished, whenever they wished—not only when they sought to reproduce, but *all the time!*"

"No! Even the animals . . ."

"And there were wars in which nations tried to destroy each other with atomic weapons—and churches, where men would go once a week to be forgiven of their sins by an invisible and nonexistent god."

"True. The world would have been destroyed by now, and perhaps other worlds too. Men always thought in terms of exploration, conquest and destruction. First our own earth, and then the planets—they were moving in that direction. By now the entire solar system might have been destroyed in the man-made atomic fire."

"Still, it seems unnecessary to bring experiment 454 to a total halt. After all, we have it under complete control. What harm could there be in studying it further? For a while, anyway?"

"Better not let Senior Mistress hear you talking that way! Well, we have our orders. Who is going to destroy Test 454?"

Koralin said: "I will."

The women regarded her curiously.

Koralin went on, her face impassive. "Let me destroy the specimen. I feel strongly about it, and I would be serving the Senior Mistress in a direct way."

"How do you propose to do it?" asked the senior cytologist, an elderly woman of silver hair and narrow face.

"Parametrically," Koralin said. "Even the destruction of a useless specimen can be useful. I should like to make a series of tests to examine oxygen consumption in terms of brain chemistry, reducing the level of oxygen minute by minute to the point of death."

"Excellent. I see you have the correct scientific attitude, Koralin."

"Well, it occurred to me that even at this stage we might learn something about male physiology and survival resilience—and that knowledge might help medical science in some way."

"Good—but we must not delay the killing too long. The Mistress's instructions were quite precise, and they made no provision for experiment."

"One hour," said Koralin. "That's all I ask. It will give me an opportunity to make blood tests and check on brain waveforms as the oxygen content of the blood is reduced to zero."

"Very well," said the senior cytologist. "You may destroy Test 454. Let me know if you obtain any data of significant interest."

"I will," Koralin promised.

Koralin transferred the baby to a sealed oxygen chamber and regulated the flow of gas to normal intake. Several of her colleagues watched her for a few minutes, but presently they grew bored and wandered off to pursue their own tasks. Koralin found herself alone with the male child.

There was no hurry. What she was about to do required the utmost calm and self-possession, and it was essential that she should not be observed. She busied herself for a few minutes with instruments, occasionally moving over to the oxygen chamber and examining the baby, as if making a methodical physical survey. Then she crossed to a screened annex containing drugs and chemicals and leisurely, though carefully, filled a hypodermic syringe from a tiny rubber-capped green phial. She injected the contents of the syringe into the baby. It cried for an instant in outraged anger, then became quiescent and, after a few moments, stiffened into a wax doll.

Satisfied, she scanned the laboratory. The other women appeared to be engrossed in their work, engaged at the incubation racks and peering into microscopes, carrying on the routine of cytology and embryology as if the research program were unchanging and eternal. They had not yet realized that it had come to an abrupt stop—that there would be no further experiments to manufacture a male embryo. Their minds were so drilled that they would continue in the pattern of their work until the official order of negation arrived. Cease work. Why? Because we are no longer interested in creating a male. Why? Because we succeeded and learned that our kind of society would be better off without it. Therefore further research along such lines has no purpose and no possible justification.

There was no longer time for further introspective reflection. The moment for action had come. Quickly she opened her white smock so that it hung shapelessly around her, then opened the oxygen chamber and lifted the baby out, slipping it beneath the loose smock. As an additional precaution she crossed to the records annex and picked up a sheaf of papers, which she held in front of her. Then, feeling that her burden was reasonably well disguised, she walked swiftly from the laboratory to the domestic quarters. In her own room she laid the baby gently upon the bed.

Staring thoughtfully down at it, she was struck suddenly by the foolhardiness of what she had done. Without premeditation and with only a minimum of hurried planning she had embarked on the first dangerous step of what she could only envisage as the absolutely impossible: the kidnapping and care of the only male child in the world in defiance of ruthless totalitarian authority. Anxiety hardened the faint lines around her brown eyes, and her long triangular face, usually ascetic and unemotional, reflected a dark shadow of apprehension. She stroked her cropped black hair with nervous fingers while her mind was busy making a tentative reconnaissance of the immediate future.

One thing was certain: She could not afford to remain in the building a moment longer than was absolutely necessary. Once the alarm had been raised, the security police would be mobilized in strength. Every second of delay meant increasing jeopardy—no time to stop and think—it was imperative to keep on the move. One could always think while moving.

She hunted in a cupboard for a large sheet of brown paper and a plastic shopping bag. With careful hands she lifted the inert baby and slipped the paper beneath it, then proceeded to make a compact parcel which she packed gently into the bottom of the plastic bag. On top of the paper bundle she placed a folded crimson cloak.

Finally, satisfied that the carrier bag was to all appearances innocent enough, she picked it up and left the room, making her way with as much nonchalance as she could muster to the swift silent elevator that led to ground level and the open city.

There was no trouble with the security guards at the main exit. They knew her well as an important member of the scientific staff, and the shopping bag was too ordinary to arouse suspicion. She walked for two blocks, then took a velocab and traveled to Kincross Station, a central terminal for the high-speed monorail trains that covered the country on atomic jet units.

She bought a ticket to the city of Birm, where she had trusted friends who, like herself, had always quietly and without fuss resisted the arrogant regimentation of a society which they had all recognized as being in the grip of perversion neurosis—which was by no means so stable and controlled as the government imagined.

The Controller of Internal Security switched off the videophone and pressed a green button on the intercom panel.

"Get me the Senior Mistress of Applied Cytology in Zone Four."

"Yes, Mistress."

Fifteen seconds of silence, then a metallic voice through the intercom loudspeaker grill.

"Applied Cytology. Senior Mistress speaking."

The Controller faded up the video screen. A flaccid, square-jawed face stared at her from beyond the rectangular glass panel.

"Code six," said the Controller curtly.

The image on the screen glanced downwards. Unseen fingers moved an unseen switch. Scrambler circuits clicked into operation to render the conversation indecipherable at all intermediate points between the two terminals.

"I have received an alarming report," said the Controller. "It involves you."

"Indeed?"

"And Test 454."

The Mistress smiled a little. "Test 454 has been destroyed."

"Are you certain?"

"I gave the order myself."

"And you witnessed the destruction and confirmed the death of the specimen?"

"Not personally. It was unnecessary. The staff of the cytological laboratory can be trusted to obey orders."

"All of them?"

The Mistress's face became a little smug. "With one exception—a woman named Cordelia who proved to have certain reversionist ideas. I have arranged for a course of hypno-orientation. She will not return to the laboratory."

"Supposing I were to tell you that Test 454 was not destroyed."

Another smile—somewhat shallower. "That would be highly improbable."

The Controller said nothing, but just watched the screen with inscrutable eyes. The smile of the image faded slowly.

"The specimen must have been destroyed within minutes of my leaving the laboratory. I am confident that it was done swiftly and efficiently. Naturally, I could not wait—there was the woman named Cordelia to escort to a place of supervision."

"I think," said the Controller gently, "that you had better come here. There are things we must talk about."

The image of the Mistress froze. Fear darkened her eyes for an instant. "You mean . . . ?"

"I mean, Mistress, that Test 454 is still alive. Not only that, but the specimen has been removed from the laboratory. And that means you are in serious trouble."

"I will come right away," said the Mistress faintly.

After the image had faded from the screen, the Controller thumbed the intercom again.

"I want to send a broadcast message to all security units and headquarters throughout the world. Message begins. Code six. Priority Emergency. Tactics urgent military. Subject act of utmost subversion. Text: Two hours ago the living body of a male specimen child

developed from an experimental embryo was stolen
from a cytological laboratory in Lon, Zone Four, by a
woman named Koralin (databank dossier CYTUK/
KOR/4472/300561/RK/70742). This woman must be
apprehended without fail, using all *breakthru* emergency security tactics. The specimen, which has not
been accorded mortic classification as human, must be
instantly destroyed and incinerated, by full authority
of the world computer brain network."

She paused and referred to a folder of papers.

"In a moment I shall give you a detailed physical
description of the woman Koralin and an indication of
her probable movements. Following this, an immediate
total security check is to be placed on all airports, sea-
ports, monorail stations, road tollgates, and provision-
ing centers. All vehicles entering and leaving all towns
and cities are to be stopped and searched. All pedestri-
ans carrying parcels, bundles or bags of any kind are
to be halted and searched. This is a *breakthru* emergency operation."

A pause; then: "Here is a detailed description of the
woman Koralin . . ."

Koralin began unwrapping the bundle. Her hands
moved slowly, methodically. With a theatrical touch
she kept the contents covered by the paper until she
was ready to perform the final unveiling ceremony, then
she said: "The world brain decided, after many weeks
of careful consideration, that *this* should be destroyed."

She unveiled the baby in a crackling flourish of paper. "It is a male child," she said, unable to conceal
a nuance of pride in her voice. "Test 454 is the official
designation. The microcytology transfer was performed
by a woman named Cordelia. When the embryo started
to grow, we took over."

Her friend, Aubretia, incredulous and vaguely horrified, inspected the pale still body of the baby from
a distance, her fingers touching her cheek in abject
uncertainty.

"But . . . it's *dead!*"

"No. Merely unconscious—in a kind of cataleptic
state. I injected paracain. The child will sleep for about
thirty hours."

"Then what?"

"The Senior Mistress of Cytology this morning gave
the order for the destruction of this child. You realize
what that could have meant?"

"No . . ."

"It would have meant the end of all hope for the
perverted and neurotic society in which we live. It
would have been the final act of despotism establishing
for all time the robot state—female robots working to
the orders of electronic computers. This baby"—Koralin touched the infant gently—"could be the savior of
womankind."

"Savior?"

"I realize I am talking about things that you may
not fully understand, but believe me, Aubretia, what
I am saying to you is the truth. The last man died
some five hundred years ago. Women would have died
off too if scientists had not learned how to perpetuate
the human species by artificial means—but a monosexual society must of necessity be a perverted society,
conforming to distorted patterns of behavior and for
that reason all the more susceptible to regimentation.
You must have heard of the parthenogenetic adaptation
syndrome. It is a disease, and we are diseased, all of
us, and we shall go on being diseased until the end of
time—unless . . ."

"Unless," Aubretia repeated, not comprehending but
sensing the ominous implications of the other woman's
argument.

"Unless we turn the clock back five hundred years.

Unless we reintroduce a male sex and revert to a normal way of living and reproducing."

"But would it be normal?"

Koralin smiled grimly. "Study ancient history. Consider nature as a whole. Then look around you at the world *we* know—laboratories, experiments in human embryology, fertility centers, induced parthenogenesis, the syndrome, cultivated Lesbianism. Don't you feel that something is missing?"

"No—but sometimes yes. I have a feeling, but I can't define it."

"Would you want the world to go on in this way for the next ten thousand years?"

Aubretia spread her hands uncertainly. "I don't think I shall have any feelings about it a hundred years from now."

"That is the voice of deep hypnosis, Aubretia. There was a time when you were concerned about the state of the world today—sufficiently concerned to risk your future and even your life."

"I don't remember."

"But you will. I'll help you to remember."

Aubretia walked slowly across the room to the window and looked out into the night with its twinkling firmament of colored neons. "All I know is that you have brought here a male experimental specimen which should have been destroyed. Why, Koralin? Tell me why?"

"Because a point in time has been reached when human affairs, human evolution, could change—once only, and for the last time. I was assigned to destroy the child. I volunteered to, deliberately, in order to be in a position to protect the child. This is the first and last male child we shall ever see in the rest of eternity."

"But you can't get away with it, Koralin. Once they find out, there is no corner of the world where you will be safe. They will seek you out and they will take the child and destroy it anyway, and perhaps you too. What will you have gained?"

Koralin shook her head. "He is only a tiny creature, easy to hide and easy to nourish. I can't do it alone, Aubretia, but a group of us could conceal him and keep him alive to grow and mature."

"How long would that take?"

"Sixteen, eighteen years—perhaps less."

Aubretia sighed wearily. "You know it's impossible. There are security agents everywhere."

"We should have to escape—move out of the city, perhaps to some other part of the world. In a small community, beyond the reach of security."

"There is no such place."

"But there is, Aubretia. Central Africa, Siberia, Antarctica . . ."

"But how could you raise a child under such conditions?"

Koralin's lips were pressed into a stubborn line. "By constant care and attention. A dozen of us could do it, and the movement would spread and grow strong. As the child matured there would be thousands of us, and when he was old enough to effect fertilization, then there would be more male children—and they too would grow and mature."

"You are dreaming, Koralin. You could never take the child more than half a dozen paces outside this building. . . ."

"There are ways and means. I would have to stay here for a few days to make plans and contact other women whom I know would be sympathetic."

Aubretia crossed to the other woman and regarded her solemnly. "You're a courageous woman, Koralin, but what you say is impossible. You are thinking in terms of starting some kind of colony in opposition to the existing world authority and in defiance of the world computer brain." A coldly considered pause. "It couldn't possibly work."

"It could, given faith."

"Faith in what? I'm a borderline case, I know. You tell me I was once treated for subversion—but I am what I am, and my faith stops short at the Department of Mortic Administration. If I really thought you had the slightest chance I might support you, Koralin, but frankly . . ." She shook her head disconsolately.

"Then may I stay here for a day—two days?" Koralin asked.

"With the male specimen?" Aubretia took a deep breath and made her decision. "I'm sorry, Koralin. It's a risk I dare not take. If I was guilty of subversion at one time, then it is certain that I am under security surveillance. It wouldn't be fair to you, or to me or the child."

The disappointment that darkened Koralin's eyes was suppressed almost immediately. She glanced down at the baby, still lying white and motionless on the table, but there was no softening of the hard determined lines around her mouth.

"Aubretia, I appeal to you."

"I'm sorry. I must ask you to go."

"Well, then—have you a car?"

Aubretia nodded.

"May I take it for a few days. I'll have it returned to you."

"They'll be stopping all cars."

"I'll take a chance. I may be able to cut across country in the outer suburbs."

Aubretia frowned. "I wouldn't want the car damaged."

"Aren't you prepared to make any kind of sacrifice?"

"For what? I can't believe in your dream, Koralin. If they arrest you in my car then I too shall be in trouble. I don't want to be involved. All I ask is to be left in peace."

"Very well. We'll leave you in peace."

Carefully Koralin wrapped up the inert child in the

sheet of paper and placed it in the plastic bag, spreading the crimson cloak on top. Her movements were methodical and unhurried. When she had finished she took the bag by its handle and moved towards the door.

She turned finally towards Aubretia and said: "Give me one hour, please."

"One hour?"

"Before you call the police."

Aubretia's pallid face sagged despondently. "Koralin, please trust me, in spite of what I may have done in the forgotten past. I shan't call the police."

"Thank you," said Koralin simply. Clutching the bag tightly, she went through the doorway into the darkness of an unguessable future.

After Koralin had gone, Aubretia went out onto the balcony overlooking the city. Her mind was now tranquil enough, for she had already dismissed Koralin and her strange quest as an irrelevancy. The streets below, warmly floodlit, were peaceful, and the lights of the tall buildings were calm and colorful. There was nothing to indicate the tightening web of security —indeed, the very concept of security might have been a myth.

For the good citizen, she thought, life is pleasant. Security is for the misfits, the agitators, the wild dreamers who try to undermine the stability of the State— women like Koralin, for instance, who not only pursue their own tortuous antisocial concepts but also seek to drag others into the engulfing vortex of their intrigues. As for the male child, it was nothing but a freak. The human species had progressed far beyond the crude condition of heterosexuality; reproduction was now an exact science. Society was stable, the future secure, and the good citizen had nothing to fear.

Unless . . . Another horrific thought stabbed needle-like at her brain. Supposing they discovered that Koralin had been here, in her apartment, with the male child? If they caught her they would inevitably interrogate her and check on her every movement since she escaped from the laboratory in Lon. The truth would be bound to emerge. Aubretia, they would say: the woman with the record; two years ago she underwent hypnotic reorientation for subversion, and now she has done it again—she has harbored a criminal and allowed her to escape without notifying security. And they would confer with the Department of Mortic Revenue and decide whether her potential usefulness in society was enough to justify continual survival, or whether this second lapse merited judicial euthanasia.

Panic seized her heart with icy fingers. Chilled and trembling, she hurried into the thermostatic warmth of the apartment and pressed the red button on the videophone.

"Please," she said urgently, "get me security, quickly. . . ."

The Controller of Internal Security was writing a confidential memorandum to her immediate superior in the government Ministry. It was to be delivered by hand. The memo stated:

We have not yet, after ten days, located the Koralin woman or Test 454. While we believe she is still in Birm, other reports suggest that a large number of women are now involved, and they may be acting as a chain to smuggle the specimen out of the country. I have therefore alerted all foreign governments and requested their cooperation.

There are some signs of spreading disaffection. Since experiments in microcytology on male gametes have been prohibited, cytologists throughout the world are protesting and actually questioning central authority and the validity of decisions made by the world com-

puter brain network. Some are actually demanding that Test 454 be allowed to survive and be accorded human status. The poison seems to be creeping into the civil population, too, particularly in Asia, where the syndrome is probably weaker than elsewhere. Already a number of attempts have been made to sabotage units of the world brain network and related public utilities and government offices.

We are not anticipating such disorder in this country, but we nevertheless have to be prepared for contingencies. Consequently I have ordered a full security mobilization. However, apart from a vague air of restlessness, especially among the scientific strata of our society, there have been no demonstrations.

It seems strange to me that such a small thing could unbalance a perfectly planned and stable society. I put forward the view (for governmental policy consideration) that stability may be geared in some way to purpose and direction, and that perhaps one stabilizing factor was the research into the synthetic creation of a human male. Without that focal point of endeavor, like the nucleus of a cell, it may be that a society tends to lose its purpose and coherence and therefore to disintegrate. The psychology of a social perversion neurosis is very complex.

However, the situation is well under control. As soon as we have apprehended the Koralin woman and recovered possession of Test 454, we shall be able to enforce complete social stability once more. Until then . . .

The explosion flung one of the tall windows of the room inwards in a cascade of glass splinters. The building shook as if in the steel grip of an earthquake. Alarmed but wary, the Controller crossed cautiously to the shattered window.

There was something wrong with the sky. Towards the east the deepening purple of approaching night was aflame with a livid orange stain. An alarm bell sounded remotely, echoing from the smooth walls of the high buildings lining the cavernous streets. And as she watched, incandescence burst into spontaneous life farther south, in the direction of the Department of Statistics. Then came another shuddering explosion, more alarm bells, and in the road far below the distant murmur of excited voices.

She stared in horror at the glowing stains of destruction in the sky. "It has started," she told herself. "And all because of one male child. This is the end of all things. . . ."

But a quiet voice buried deep in the twisted darkness of her mind whispered: "This is only the beginning. . . ."

Chapter Five

"You have to remember," said the Senior Lecturer in Bioeconomic History, "that all human society is potentially unstable. No matter how definitive and crystallized the regime may appear to be, it involves the conflict of opposites. Indeed, the stronger the regime, the more vulnerable it is to violent disruption. Stability is mere equilibrium, with opposing forces balanced on a knife edge."

About twenty students occupied the auditorium of the half-empty lecture theater, young females in their late teens. All looked remarkably alike, which was to be expected as parthenogenesis tightened its inflexible grip on what was left of the mechanics of human reproduction. The lecturer was a much older woman—tall, lean and angular, with cropped purple-lacquered hair. She wore a short translucent cape which covered her gilt-sprayed breasts. The students also wore capes, but they had been rolled up around the neck in the form of a collar and secured with a silver pin and chain.

The air in the theater was warm and soporific. Beyond the long horizontal window the sun threw a forest of white monolithic skyscrapers into incandescence and cast long pointing shadows across the highways and green parklands of the city. Faint streamers of high cirrus cloud diluted the intense blue of the sky. It was an unkind day for concentration and study, and even the lecturer's flat intonation seemed to lack enthusiasm for the reversionist revolution, which was the subject of the discourse.

"The ruling hierarchy tends to act to maintain the status quo out of self-preservation," she continued. "It will, in yielding to pressure from underneath, introduce only such social and economic changes as will in the long run consolidate and strengthen its political security and standing. But beneath the imposed establishment pattern the contrary revolutionary pattern is continuous. The one is, as it were, superimposed on the other—and it is one of the basic tenets of political and economic dynamics that when two opposing patterns are superimposed, a third pattern emerges which is an integrated function of both but totally different from either. That is why the actual implemented policies of revolutionary governments invariably differ from the professed, and promised, policies of revolutionary movements before they acquire power—and it matters not whether you are thinking in terms of the totalitarian state or the democracy."

At the back of the theater, near the window, a girl named Lycia was looking sidelong through half-closed eyes at the sunlit towers of the metropolis, though hardly seeing them, for her mind was focused elsewhere. The lecturer's droning voice was little more than background jamming to her own idle thoughts, with occasional intelligible phrases breaking through to her drifting awareness. But in their own way her thoughts were, in their more naive fashion, as important a contribution to the science of bioeconomics as were the words being uttered by the woman on the rostrum.

I wish I were an albino like Crinila (she was thinking)—to be beautiful without having to use lacquers and sprays and cosmetics. And white hair, like snow, and pink eyes, and a skin so smooth as to be almost transparent. And yet, what advantage is there in being

so beautiful when it arouses envy and spite? They say
that Crinila is a freak because of a genetic malfunc-
tion, and that she will never be allowed to reproduce,
and in the end her strain will die out.

But why? Because her strain is substandard, according to the Ministry of Eugenic Control, and we must
all be standardized, like those buildings of the metropolis. Yet they all want Crinila. When it comes to erotic
play Crinila and the other albinos like her are always
in demand—I suppose because they are different from
the rest of us. There must be some significance in that.

"Now you will understand the explanation given in
the world's official history books for the unprecedented
insurrection that spread like a fireflash around the
planet following the creation and abduction of Test
454—that is, the male child," the Senior Lecturer went
on. "It is interesting to note that the books contain no
reference to the parthenogenetic syndrome, nor to the
perversion neurosis of society as a whole, although
these conditions still obtained. The emphasis is on instability rather than stability—the emergence of a new
social order from the blending of the constituent patterns. That process is still under way today, but under
careful planning control. It is known as the reversionist
flux.

"The most significant factor, from the point of view
of the governments and administrations of the time,
was that the reversionist insurrection originated among
the scientific community—among those women whose
minds should have been dominated by logic rather
than emotion. This might have been predicted, but was
not. In retrospect the fallacy is clear.

"The scientists were those women who knew at least
some of the truth about the so-called parthenogenetic
syndrome and realized, if only in part, the true nature
of the dilemma facing a unisexual society. Despite con-
ditioning and indoctrination from childhood, they were
able to attain objective and perceptive attitudes, seeing

and understanding the human problem in the wider
context of terrestrial biology as a whole.

"Until the male child had been synthesized in the
form of Test 454, it was a problem with only an imaginary solution. But from the moment the male child
drew its first breath the solution became real. Now,"
—the lecturer paused and scanned her audience as if
to make sure none was asleep—"to have destroyed Test
454, as was decreed by law, would have been tanta-
mount to multiplying the basic equation by zero, and
you all know what that means. It would have canceled
out any real solution and restored the status quo of the
imaginary solution. And the world computer had, of
course, been programmed to maintain the status quo."

I suppose, thought Lycia, that if nature had wanted
all women to be identical she would have arranged it
so in the first place. And yet, if you look at the animal
and vegetable worlds, you see differentiation and vari-
egation on an infinite scale. An explantory word flashed
into her mind. Cross-fertilization. But that involved a
bisexual form of reproduction and no longer applied to
homo sapiens as a species. It seemed strange to her
that the women of today knew so very little of the
long-dead world of men—as though all records, books
and pictures had been destroyed or locked away in
secret archives.

And yet it was the avowed object of the reversionist
technocracy in which she lived to restore the male sex,
but it would take a long time—perhaps many centuries
of time. Meanwhile, life went on just the same. What
was so different about the world before and after the
revolution? She was too young to remember—or perhaps there was nothing worth remembering, anyway.

The Senior Lecturer continued: "The destruction of
Test 454 might, had it happened, have been accepted
as a *fait accompli* with little or no protest, had not
the world federal government issued an edict forbidding all further research work on the creation of a

viable male embryo. That was the broad red line drawn
across the scientific log book. The computer had decided, in its wisdom, that the male sex was unnecessary and undesirable—but the scientists knew that the
computer did not possess wisdom. It was no more than
a fast calculating machine, devoid of the attributes of
judgment or imagination. It was a robot obeying instructions fed into it by programs that had been
written by motivated human females, and its impersonal
printout was merely an electronic computation of the
input data in accordance with the program rules. It
was a game with political undertones.

"While the mass of womankind held the computer
in awe—to many it was a kind of all-knowing god—
the scientists knew better. Even so, they were not anti-
computer in attitude any more than one could reasonably be, say, anti-typewriter or anti-adding-machine. It
all depended on whose finger was pressing the keys, or,
in computer terms, whose brain was compiling the programs.

"The most obvious interpretation of the computed
decision to destroy Test 454 was that the move had
been designed not so much to preserve the stability of
a perverted society as to maintain the ascendancy of the
political hierarchy ruling that society. That, plus the
official abandonment of any further research into male
embryo synthesis, was a positive indication that the
political establishment, worldwide, liked its existing
power and had no intention whatever of permitting
any kind of competition—for all time, if need be. It is
a pattern that has been repeated many times throughout history, and it always fails in the long term because
biology is more potent that politics, and the underdog
has a stronger motivation for survival than the complacent top dog. Number two invariably possesses more
dynamism than number one—like the lava inside a
volcano."

I ought to be paying attention to the lecturer, Lycia

thought, turning her eyes back to the rostrum and the angular woman in the translucent cape. But she is telling me what I already know, except that she is using the jargon of science to make it sound—well, authoritative and official. When I am older I may have to teach others the same truths concealed in the same jargon. At least it makes a change to be taught by a living human instead of an electronic teaching machine, with its programmed microfilms and tapes—and that wasn't so many years ago. It is almost as if they are slowly turning the clock back, so that humans communicate more with each other than with machines. The word is reversionism—but reversion to what, and in preparation for what? Perhaps they themselves do not even know.

It all has to do with the male child—at least, that is what they tell us over and over again. But how can the structure and beliefs of a vast complex society be dramatically changed by one tiny infant? Yes, there was a parallel, in a way, nearly three thousand years ago, and that child, too, was supposed to be the product of a parthenogenetic virgin birth. Impossible, of course, for parthenogenetic birth can only produce females, and, anyway, it was long before things such as parthenogenesis and microcytology were ever dreamed of. That child, too, was ordered to be destroyed by the State, but he was taken away and hidden. I wonder where they have hidden the new male child of our day—always supposing he exists at all.

The trouble is that one cannot even trust our enlightened reversionary establishment to tell the truth, and the whole truth. A revolution may be fast and ruthless, but the metamorphosis of society from one shape into another is a long and painful process, and old mythologies and customs die slowly. I am being too impatient in a world where stoic patience has been the norm for hundreds of years.

The Senior Lecturer was still talking, but with slight-

ly more animation, Lycia thought. This was probably
because the discourse appeared to be descending from
the higher realms of bioeconomic theorizing to historical fact, and the lecturer was actually posing a
question:

"What, then, actually did happen after the comatose
body of the male child was abducted from the secret
cytological laboratory by Koralin—a tested and trusted
junior scientist of the female autocracy? First, the world
computer brain network buzzed frantically with digital
activity, issuing directives formulated by programs that
had not been compiled to foresee such a dramatic contingency. Among those directives was the fateful one
prohibiting further research into male embryo synthesis.

"Desperate attempts were made by the administration to amend existing programs and write new ones,
but the effort was time-consuming, and as each day
passed the situation changed, making many of the program modifications obsolescent before they had been
completed. It proved to be one of the very few 'real-
time' situations that could *not* be put 'on-line' to the
computer for immediate decisive processing, and so the
world computer network became discredited almost
overnight, and decision-making was relegated to the
lower and more emotional level of the human brain.

"This apparent abdication of ultimate authority by
the machine created a vacuum which sucked in anarchy,
and that in turn provoked a quasi-military backlash
from the Establishment. The computer had failed to
solve an urgent problem—how, then, could it possibly
be solved by those who accepted their policies and
directives from the computer? The only practical solution was one of the oldest known to mankind—the use
of immediate and ruthless force to suppress the insurrection.

"The result was neither a revolution nor a civil war,
but rather an extended riot which spread swiftly across
the globe. It was the first of its kind on an international

scale for nearly half a millennium, and it took the centralized world federal administration by surprise. Individual government, though skilled enough in 'balancing the syndrome' by using the sciences of indoctrination and what is known as 'mind-bending,' were simply not geared for armed conflict. That kind of thing had died out with the last man, and after a long era of peace, military weapons of any significant scale were virtually unknown. Even manual small arms were designed to fire anesthetic pellets rather than bullets; while generally effective for crowd control, they lacked the life-or-death deterrent power necessary in a more serious situation of determined riot. It was ironic, but perhaps fitting, that the reappearance of man in the shape of the male child should instantly bring violent strife back into a world of long-standing peace and contentment."

At least she didn't use the word "happiness," Lycia thought. "Contentment" was apt enough—the contentment of the grazing animal in its herd or flock, with no need to worry about the future or the past, living for today, looked after, sheltered, fed, tended and bred according to eugenic principles. Well, perhaps it wasn't quite so bad as that. True, one was conceived, delivered, nourished, trained and educated by the State, and also put to work by the State, for all industry, commerce, science and art belonged to the State. But there were relaxations, too—games and sports, both physical and intellectual, and electronic amusements in which one could live, for a few hours, a vicarious "dream life" of adventure or erotic love prerecorded on tape and played back into the brain.

And since the revolution one could form friendships and liaisons and enjoy love affairs with other women without security vetting and the possibility of a veto, and without registering for a certificate of approval. Even Crinila was now accessible, if she felt so inclined, whereas under the previous administration she would,

as an albino, have been untouchable, and might well
have died young under the cruel mortic laws.

As for the brief surge of global violence that had
shifted the balance of political power in favor of the
reversionists, you could hardly blame the male child for
that, any more than you could blame Crinila for being
what she is. The strife must have been there in latent
form all the time, like a fracture line awaiting the
slight additional pressure needed to exceed the breaking
strain.

Yet, undeniably, the male child was at the focus of
all events. For was not the unbalanced neurotic stress
under which society was forced to exist—the "syndrome," as it was called—the direct result of the disappearance of the male sex from the human world?
And was not the culture that had followed a compensation for the vacuum that could not be filled? And
would the ultimate return of the male sex, if it could
be achieved, demand a new kind of unimaginable culture, and perhaps a struggle for domination between the
sexes? It was an argument with many imponderables.

"The insurrection," the Senior Lecturer explained,
"was at first random and uncoordinated until it was
firmly taken over and led by the scientists. It was they
and their colleagues in engineering and technology who
held in their hands the only true power: the power of
control over energy supplies, electricity generation, food
synthesis, desalination plants, electronic communications, and data transmission and processing—the life-
line of the community on which all effective activity
depended.

"Like many spontaneous movements, it lacked lead-
ership in the early stages. It broke out like a mottled
rash in the main urban centers of the country, but
there was communication between the various groups
even if no common objective had yet been clearly defined. And then one began to hear more and more often
the name of a particular woman, Galinia, who seemed

to move shadowlike across Britain, and indeed Europe, tying together the tactical threads and strategic planning of the dissident units.

"It was Galinia who realized that the strength of the security reaction lay not in its puny hand-held anesthetizing weapons but in its vast dispersed databank—the computerized files and dossiers, recorded on discs, tapes and holograms, which held the personal history and mortic revenue assessment of every individual in the land. Destroy them, and you had paralyzed the vindictive brain of the administration. But it was not so simple. The files were triplicated and stored in widely different locations as insurance against loss or damage, and all were duplicated in the master files of the world brain network.

It was therefore necessary to destroy or erase the national databanks, and at the same time cut all data transmission links with the world network master files so that the information could not be retrieved until after the revolution had been won or lost. And it was this complex operation, embracing geographically throughout the world, which established Galinia as overall commander of the national revolutionary effort.

"An important part of her policy was to provide an ethic, a principle, to fight for, in order to involve the mass of the population, who were not scientists and did not understand the basic forces at work in the conflict. Without such a basic emotional driving force, any insurrection is lost before it begins. To do this it was only necessary to tell the truth, or as much of the truth as could be plausibly accepted by the indoctrinated mass of the population. Without the male sex the human race was a biological freak that should have died a natural death centuries ago, had it not been for the ingenious use of science to promote controlled virgin birth. Now, for the first and last time, it was possible to recreate the male sex and allow life to revert to what was normal. If the government would have none of it, then the people would have none of the government. And, above all, the people—that is, the scientists —were in possession of the living male child and would protect it and defend it until the end."

Lycia glanced at the theater clock. It was nearly sixteen hundred, which meant that the rather dull lecture was nearly over. Then, after a fifteen minute break, there was a final talk on matrix mathematics, which promised to be equally dull. She decided to skip it. The weather was all wrong for complex mental acrobatics—it made one feel dreamy and erotic. To prove the point she slipped one hand discreetly beneath her skirt and gently stroked her pelvis with the tips of her slender fingers. Electricity tingled briefly through the lower part of her body, and it had nothing to do with reversionism or mathematics, but rather with Crinila, and whether Crinila would be in a sportive mood this evening—always provided she were available. Which was a very good reason for leaving the university early.

"In all, the struggle lasted just over six weeks," said the Senior Lecturer, "although in other countries it dragged on for several months. The government abdicated when even the security forces began to switch their allegiance. The world federal administration was dissolved and gave way to what is now called the Central Policy Organization, whose purpose it is to coordinate the steady, but necessarily slow, progress to reversionism in all the independent nations for which it is responsible. Today we are in the first phase of that implementation. It may take five hundred years to put the clock back five hundred years, but in many respects this first phase is the most important of all."

She gathered her papers together from the rostrum. "Tomorrow I shall explain why, with particular reference to the function of the male child."

As she swept from the theater, the hands of the clock stood at precisely sixteen hundred.

Chapter Six

It took several years for a team of experts, consultants, mathematicians and computer specialists to formulate a mathematical model of the kind of adult the male child would become as it grew into puberty, adolescence, and then maturity. Even before this abstract work could start, three years had to be spent in fundamental historical research on the essential nature—anatomical, physiological and psychological—of the human male. Although computer-produced mathematical models of the human female were commonplace, and had been used to good effect in "balancing the syndrome" and so stabilizing society, no serious attempt had been made to tackle the male sex, for such an exercise, until now, would have been merely hypothetical.

Perhaps "team" of experts is a gross understatement. In all, more than five thousand specially trained women were brought together from all over the world to combine their various skills and sciences in putting together, jig-saw-like, a mathematical model of the new man by optimization of variational parameters. Only on the basis of such data could the full potential of the growing male child be put to the best and most efficient use in achieving the planned reversion of society to a state of

balanced normality—or, for those who had some mis-
givings about it, a state of comparative normality.

The operation was known as Project Alpha. It would,
it was estimated, take the best part of ten years to reach
completion, by which time the male child might reasonably be showing some signs of approaching puberty,
with the promise of imminent gamete production from
its immature testes—and that was the point at which
the immense labor involved in the theoretical ground-
work would achieve practical fruition.

The male child had not been officially named, mainly
due to the inability of various factions to reach agreement. It was felt that a creature of such vital international importance should not be given a name with
national connotations. Adam had been suggested and
widely favored for a while, but it had finally been
abandoned because logically—and all women scientists
were logical—Adam was the legendary name of the
first man, and the male child was only the second first
man. The label "Test 454" stuck for a long time, for
it possessed a remote, impersonal and clinical quality
which harmonized with the nature of the mathematical
model on which all were working. Even when the child
was no longer an infant, they still referred to him as
"it"—a habit which persisted for most of the first
decade. There is little doubt in retrospect that most
of the scientists tended to regard the child during its
early years of life as little more than an absorbing experiment for which, because of its political motivations,
unlimited funds were available.

In the end, as the model progressed the male child
became increasingly identified with Project Alpha, so
that, almost as if by tacit consent, he became known
simply as "Alpha"—and this, in an abbreviated form,
became "Alph." To the scientists of that age there
seemed nothing inappropriate or undignified in a name
that sounded like Alf. There was no official christening
ceremony; the name stuck by common usage. Alph had

become a named person, though still referred to mainly as "it."

The relationship between Project Alpha and Alpha was, in the simplest terms, rather like that of blueprint to the final product. Data had to be processed and integrated from many different sources on a number of levels. Fundamentally, there was Alph, and outside Alph was the sum total of his environment, which included the entire female population of the world. Between Alph and the environment was the "interface" through which Alph impinged upon his environment, and vice versa. Such interface interactions had to be modeled and predicted in a permutation and combination fashion for all imaginable states of Alph and environment, both separately and simultaneously.

Alph itself was problem enough because of its immaturity. Detailed biopsy and DNA electron microscope analyses could indicate probable physical development, and glandular tests suggested certain possibilities of personality and temperament, but these were subject to the constraints exercised by variable environmental conditions. In fact, all functions were variables: The development and ultimate nature of Alph would react to changes in environment in all its aspects, just as the environment itself, particularly in terms of deliberately controlled parameters, would need to change or be changed in response to unpredicted variations in the maturing Alph.

The object was to create an optimum Alph within an optimum environment, or, in other words, to balance a simultaneous equation with an infinite number of variables. Not even a battery of the world's most powerful computers could hope to print out a definitive solution, and the best that could be achieved in practice would necessarily be a series of converging approximations. To develop the software alone, even though the high-speed hardware was available and standing by, would take years of unremitting effort and teamwork.

To illustrate the intricacy of the task, some five years after the revolution a preliminary set of handbooks was published in a limited and confidential edition for the guidance of the scientists concerned. It comprised twenty thick volumes of more than one thousand pages each, under the overall title: *Project Alpha—Analyses and Optimization by Variational Parameters*. And that was merely the preamble to the complete handbook, which would be written and compiled as work progressed, and was expected to amount to more than two hundred similar volumes.

And as for the cause of all this intense and costly activity, the small chunk of human being informally labeled Alph, *it* was enjoying, if that was the word, the flattering process of being scientifically optimized by the world's finest brains and machines in a secret location, protected by the most stringent security measures and life-support monitoring systems in all human history. Alphaville, as the site became known, was a fair-sized purpose-built township which might have been located anywhere on the planet. Invisible from the air, it was equally undetectable by radar, laser or infrared probe systems. For the population of some five thousand female scientists and a superstructure of administrators, it was a self-contained and self-sustaining prison to which they were confined until the successful completion of the project. Logistics and communications with the outside world were arranged over a series of multiplicated relay links through which passed code-consigned supplies and information, and even heads of State were as ignorant as their own people, though better informed on the improving state of the art in the one nursery in the world that really mattered.

Of the five thousand specialists working on Project Alpha, only twenty had direct physical access to the male child. They had been hand-picked, meticulously vetted, and intensively trained for what was rated as the most responsible job of modern civilization—indeed,

of all time. For the rest of womankind, knowing only
what the administration chose to announce in the form
of infrequent and cautiously worded progress reports,
life went on much the same as before, but with the
incremental introduction of new liberties and privileges
and the phased withdrawal of civil security measures.
The Department of Mortic Revenue had the legal teeth
pulled and so lost its bite. True, life for most was still
boring and doctrinaire, with heavy emphasis on political
reeducation and reorientation, and it happened so slowly, like the long dragging thaw of a glacier creeping im-
perceptibly from the summit of a frigid mountain.

As a policy Project Alpha had its impatient op-
ponents, but they were not scientists and held no
practical power and influence. To them, Utopia, like
all Utopias, seemed a long time in the making and often
appeared to recede and dissolve mirage-like as one
drew steadily nearer to it. For all that, there was little
discontent, and as the years rolled by with monotonous
sameness, a new generation of parthenogenetic children
grew into adolescence and early adulthood with a different philosophy of life and a new table of priorities—
and it all hinged on Alph, the male child, concealed,
unseen and unheard. Alph, at that time, was undoubtedly
the most important creation in the universe, to which
all other considerations were subordinated. No male
child had ever had it so good—or had he?

The infantile years of Alph were much the same as
any female baby raised in a State nursery anywhere
in the world: the white and chrome and vivid colors
of rooms, the soft glow of luminous ceilings; the thermostatically controlled warmth and the almost inaudible
whine of airconditioning and humidifying plant; the
toys, devised by psychologists and therefore rather

boring, and the fluffy cosy tops in the shape of animals, not devised by psychologists, which proved more popular and had to be constantly sterilized in the interests of continuous hygiene.

And the enormous open space outside the nursery block, with the bright blue ceiling sometimes animated by drifting clusters of white cotton wool, and a central incandescent orb which was warm to the skin and too intense to look at directly; and the soft though slightly prickly green carpet on the floor, surrounded, at a distance, by myriad blobs of rainbow colors among a tangle of green that protruded from a narrow brown border and sometimes nodded and swayed when the air moved and was cool to the skin.

All these things had an explanation, but Alph had not yet reached the age when questions and answers were either necessary or possible. For him the outside world was visual and tactile—it consisted of light, darkness, color, shapes, and surfaces that were rough or smooth. There were also sounds and noises, some soothing and some alarming, but they were different because one could not hold a noise and study it in the same way that one could stare at a twinkling colored light or stroke and clutch the friendly fur of a teddy bear.

The noises were random, transient events most made by the white-coated and white-masked giants who came into his room and did things to him from time to time. Sometimes they did nice things, like stuffing food and drink into his mouth, and sometimes unpleasant things, like popping him into a container of warm water and wrapping uncomfortable wads of cloth around his bottom. Occasionally they jabbed needles into his arms and legs and made him scream, and they were forever touching and poking him with contraptions connected to tubes and wires and attaching strange objects to his head.

They made most of the noises with their mouths,

and they seemed to make them to each other, but at times a face would come close to his and utter incomprehensible sounds directly to him. He was not to know that these strange giants were simply a larger version of himself; apart from sensations of pain and pleasure, discomfort and comfort, he was not really aware of himself at all.

Certain things that could be seen and touched and heard over and over again became familiar by repetition, and when they were not associated with pain or discomfort they pleased him, and he wanted them to come back, and was happy when they did so. In such a way, selectively, he earmarked those features of the curious outside world which gave him a feeling of safety and security. Among the giants, some seemed to offer more security than others, and he liked them better. Others he hated. Among those he liked were a few who picked him up and fondled him and held him close to them, and made soothing friendly noises with their mouths. That was as close as Alph was ever likely to get to true mother-love.

When he was old enough and had learned to walk and make simple inarticulate sounds approximating elementary speech, the giants dressed him in a skirt and roll-up cape and sandals, after the fashion of the women of the day. This was no arbitrary and unimaginative decision; it had been made only after long painstaking research into the history of male attire through the ages. Apart from a few transitory phases between identifiable cultures, it was evident that males and females had dressed differently, partly for functional and partly for what might be termed "sex-plumage" reasons. That, however, had been in the long-dead bisexual era, when there had been as many men as women in the world and there was a valid motive in differentiation of dress. In a totally female world, however, there could be a psychological hazard in putting Alph into something that looked quite different from the uniform worn by everybody else: It might single him out in his own mind as an eccentric, or a freak, or subnormal, or privileged—all undesirable reactions. He would need to feel that he "belonged" to the rest of humanity and was one of them, even though he would know soon enough that in certain important respects his body had been differently designed. Consequently, the young Alf, when dressed, looked exactly like any young girl of equivalent age from a State nursery.

Then came the lessons—the carefully prepared curriculum of education and training, prescribed and detailed step by step by the computers. First, communication. Until Alph could talk, listen, read and write, no real progress could be made—not that anyone had really defined what was meant by progress, since it would have been perfectly feasible in a strict scientific sense to keep him uneducated and inarticulate, purely as a source of male gametes for the greater worldwide experiment that was to come. That could well indeed have been the coldly clinical attitude of the former administration, but the reversionists had shed much of the impersonal robot-like veneer characteristic of their predecessors, even daring to exhibit sentiment and emotion beyond the permitted limitations of approved Lesbian liaisons.

Alph, for his part, had no clearly defined focus for emotion. He belonged, it seemed to him, to a number of giants, some of whom were more possessive than others. There was no singular mother image, but rather a plurality of mothers, and certainly no hint or conception of a father, whatever that might have meant, either to himself or his female mentors; for his father had been a microscopic genetic thread of DNA proteins transplanted by microsurgery from a dead spermatazoon of a dead man. In this respect, therefore, his rearing and upbringing was abnormal from the start, even though the few scientists and psychologists selected to supervise his day-to-day development sincerely believed that they were providing as normal an ambience as possible. In practice, it was anything but that.

The male child advanced into early puberty, and the computers buzzed with accelerating activity as they evaluated the immense variety of options on which strategic planning decisions had to be made. Already at the age of eight signs of latent sexual interest, though inward orientated, had become evident to observers watching through one-way polarized glass panels and via concealed video recording cameras. There were the first fumbling and uncomprehending essays in juvenile masturbation, confirmed by new modulation frequencies appearing in the EEG records of brain waveforms. No attempt was made to interfere with this perfectly natural form of diversion, but swabs taken of emissions of semen in the early exercises revealed no trace of spermatozoa. Blood samples revealed the first hints of the presence of gonadotropic hormones. It became only too clear that Alph junior, still dressed as a little girl, was on the point of entering the long and difficult period of conversion into Alph senior—an arduous period, for which a massive computer-ordained program of systematic work had been laid down. A growing air of excitement and tension became apparent among the dedicated staff of Alphaville as Phase Two of Project Alpha drew nearer to implementation. The only person aware of the change in atmosphere was Alph himself, whose own personal excitement and tension, such as it was, was of a more introverted and narcissistic nature.

In political terms, the theory and policy of reversionism was about to be put to the practical test, and on the results depended the pattern, and indeed the purpose, of the human species for centuries and millennia to come.

Chapter Seven

The Central Executive Committee of the Project Alpha Supervisory Council in Alphaville consisted of four senior scientists of the highest standing in the spheres of biology, in its widest sense, and psychology. A fifth member, Koralin, enjoyed a concessionary co-opted position—a privilege granted in recognition of her vital role in abducting Test 454 from the secret laboratory in Lon and thus unwittingly launching the reversionist revolution. She did not, of course, possess the superior qualifications and experience of her elder colleagues, but it was tacitly admitted that she, of all the attendant scientists, held a genuinely emotional attachment to the male child. This attitude, though officially frowned upon in the interests of true objectivity, was useful at times in trying to ascertain what one might call "Alph's point of view" in respect of certain proposed experimental measures. Koralin was overtly protective, and this was acknowledged to be an admissible constraint.

A meeting of the Executive Council was in progress in the austere control suite overlooking the nursery gardens four stories below. The smooth green lawns framed by rainbow-splashed flower beds contrasted sharply with the grey and white of the committee room. The women sat around a black oval table with a glass top. From the ceiling a minute capsule microphone hung from a gossamer thread to record the proceedings. At the head of the table, leafing through a sheaf of typewritten notes, was Davana, the official "chairman," an aged but well-preserved woman whose grey hair had been lacquered silver. She sat lethargically, leaning forward against the table with her chin propped lazily on one hand, but her grey eyes were alert enough.

"First, the formal preamble for the record," she said in a quiet voice that was unexpectedly incisive. She recited a long code number conveying whatever was relevant to key the computerized archives—date, time, serial number, subject of meeting, attendance, and so on. Then she paused for breath and scanned her audience.

"At the age of nine years and forty-two days the male child known as Alph has finally begun to make gametes. We have been able to extract and isolate some specimens and have confirmed that they are indeed living spermatozoa."

A hiss of excitement rippled round the table like a faint breeze.

"The sample we were able to obtain was quite small, and on a statistical count it does not appear that gamete production as yet numbers more than just a few hundred head of sperm, if one may use such an expression. However, hormone activity is now at a level which suggests that output will increase very rapidly within the next few weeks, and in the course of a few months may run into millions of units."

"Then," exclaimed a bright-eyed green-haired woman named Solon, "it means that Phase Two . . ."

"Exactly. Phase Two. But first we must carry out genetic tests at DNA level to make sure that proper differentiation of the chromosomes, particularly the sex chromosomes, has occurred. That will take a little time, even with our phase-contrast electron microscope."

"But surely, Davana, normal mytosis was predicted by the computers . . ."

"In the mathematical model, yes. Here we are dealing with flesh and blood of a highly specialized type. You must remember that Test 454 was the result of precision microsurgery and refined grafting techniques from a dead gamete, and not a normal live fertilization of the ovum concerned. While we already know from biopsy tests that mytosis in the ordinary body cells is normal, we cannot necessarily assume that gamete production will follow the same desirable trend, especially in respect to the X and Y chromosomes."

A long-jawed masculine woman said in a deep voice: "In my view there will be no imperfections, but clearly we must make comprehensive checks. And, of course, the program specifies simulated fertilization tests for compatibility and non-rejection."

"That is being attended to," said Davana. "The artificial placenta is being made ready, and of course we have an adequate supply of live ova samples in serum, and more in deep freeze."

Koralin was frowning a little, for this new development in the growing up of Alph had come sooner than she had expected, even though the computers had forecast its possibility from the age of seven onwards. And the tenor of the talk created a vague anxiety within her—gametes, simulation, ova samples, artificial placenta, and so on, almost as if Alph as an individual person did not exist. However, she said nothing.

The green-haired woman, Solon, said: "According to the computers, Phase Two begins the moment live gametes are isolated and identified."

"Subject to confirmatory tests—which are in progress," Davana said in bored reproof.

"Have the Heads of State been notified?"

"They will be notified when the confirmatory tests and simulations show positive results."

"There must be no delay . . ."

"We are delaying nothing," Davana said irritably. "The rules of procedure are quite clear. If you will refer to Section 3317, Sub-section N24 in Volume 14 of the Handbook you will find the rules of procedure quite clearly laid out." As an afterthought, with a slightly sarcastic undertone, she added: "We must guard against impatience, mustn't we, Solon?"

Solon flushed at the implied reprimand. "Perhaps impatience can be justified after five centuries of enforced patience. However, I will concede that the prescribed rules of procedure must be observed."

"That is most perceptive of you," Davana remarked. Her manner made it quite clear that there was only one chairwoman and that she, in her mildly astringent fashion, was in charge of the committee.

She consulted her notes for a moment. "Phase Two is not quite so exhilarating as it sounds. It begins with a hiatus, leaving aside a very limited number of artificial insemination experiments on selected female subjects which may prove to be inconclusive, and in any case may not satisfy eugenic control requirements.

"So, the project subdivides into two parallel sectors, each hingeing upon an immensely detailed DNA and RNA analysis of a statistically valid number of gametes. These subsectors we shall call Phase 2A and Phase 2B. We here at Alphaville are concerned with Phase 2A, and the implementation of Phase 2B will be the responsibility of the Heads of State of the participating nations.

"Phase 2A is outlined in the Handbook and is elaborated in greater detail in Appendix D34, which was published about three months ago. I suggest you read it very carefully."

"I have already done so," said Solon. The others murmured likewise.

"Then I suggest you read it *again*. It is the point at which a delay may occur, but must not be allowed to occur if it is humanly possible. It is a stage of the project at which, either biochemically or electronically or by a combination of both, a reliable method must be devised of separating the X gametes from Y gametes so that one container holds the male producing spermatozoa and the other the female. It matters not if the female-producing gametes are destroyed in the process, so long as the male-producing sperms are preserved."

"There should be no problem," commented the long-jawed woman. "We were successful with animals."

"Let us say we gained experience with animals and had reasonable success with certain primates, but this is the first time with homo sapiens. There are always discrete differences in protein chemistry which even the mathematical model cannot anticipate. However, on an emergency priority basis I am confident that we shall achieve a reliable X-Y separation in a matter of—well, a few days, or perhaps weeks."

"Won't that require a regular supply of gametes in rather copious quantities?" Solon asked.

"Yes—at the statistical count stage, towards the end. But the initial steps will require only a limited number of gametes while the process is being refined, certainly well within the estimated production capacity of the Alph child. The point to remember is that we are engaged in research, not mass production. Nevertheless, the techniques we devise now will form the basis of mass production technology for years and decades to come. It is a grave responsibility."

Everybody looked suitably grave for a moment, with the exception of Koralin, whose expression of frowning unease had not perceptibly changed throughout the meeting.

"We can surely rely on our biochemists," Solon said with cheerful enthusiasm.

"That is why they were selected to work on Project Alpha," Davana retorted.

"And Phase 2B?"

"That will be carried out simultaneously with Phase 2A. Each participating government will select, by means of the most stringent genetic and eugenic tests, a number of—let us say for the want of a better word—'perfect' females, whose ova will offer optimum compatibility with the Alpha gametes. They will be segregated in special centers under conditions of maximum security. There they will be artificially inseminated, and subjected to continuous prenatal monitoring until birth is achieved."

For an instant the hint of a smile narrowed the dry lips of Davana as she added: "Each will be, in effect—indeed, in reality—the mother of one of our very first generation of new males."

"Second generation, surely," said Koralin, speaking for the first time. "Alph himself is the first generation."

"Alph is not a generation," Davana said coldly. "It was synthesized in a laboratory, not born of a woman. I think we can regard Alph as a prototype rather than a production model."

"But he is a perfectly normal boy. . . ."

Davana waved one hand airily across the table. "He was never eugenically cleared, and in any case, at one point he was classified as not of human status by the world computer."

"That was a corrupt and thoroughly discredited judgment," Koralin cried angrily, causing Davana to raise her thin eyebrows in surprise and admonition. "It was an evil and murderous judgment, and that was why I stole the child and hid it away and . . ."

"Yes, yes, yes—we know all about that," Davana interrupted impatiently. "I am not suggesting that the computer's judgment was anything more than an arrogant decree prompted by politically motivated programming. What I am trying to emphasize is that what we call Alph is not a naturally conceived organism. It is the successful and somewhat miraculous result of an experiment—one of many experiments—in transfusing certain chromosomes for a long-dead gamete into a living ovum. Alph is simply a successful experiment."

"Alph is a normal living boy," Koralin repeated stubbornly.

Davana sighed. She was not annoyed, merely bored by the other woman's emotional lack of objectivity.

"Let me draw an analogy. A gardener breeds a new species of plant—say, a hybrid rose. He then propagates and reproduces it in identical form by means of cuttings taken from the original plant. There you have the prototype and the first generation. The prototype remains the fountainhead of the resulting rose population, so to speak."

"I can't accept that analogy . . ." Koralin began, but the elder woman cut her short with another wave of her hand.

"I think, Koralin, that we are digressing. It would be better if we could talk privately after the meeting, and then perhaps I can clarify certain points of confusion which have no proper place in our agenda at this moment."

Koralin nodded with some reluctance. There was nothing to be gained by pursuing her protest, particularly as every word was being recorded on tape for filtering into the databank. Even the more liberal reversionist administration had retained a significant degree of single-mindedness in dealing with those who, in its view, unnecessarily questioned authority, and she had no desire to be expelled from Alphaville and the small boy for whom she had risked her life.

The meeting continued as if nothing had happened. Davana proceeded to explain in greater detail the itemized departmental procedures relating to Phase 2A and 2B.

Later, in Davana's private office, Koralin was invited to state her views without prejudice—and without going on official record via a bug microphone (though she could only accept Davana's word for that). In this room the furnishing and decor were less austere, though still functional. The desk, of metal and plastic, bore a tall vase of natural flowers from the nursery garden, and some pictures of urban and rural landscapes adorned the walls. Davana's manner, too, was noticeably less severe and biting, as if she were now talking over an intimate problem with a misguided and recalcitrant daughter.

"A little sentiment is not a bad thing. At least it is a human quality, but you must guard against over-sentiment, for it can betray you," Davana warned. "In a sense you are a true reversionist, but we cannot all revert so quickly, and the devolution must be very carefully controlled if we are to avoid cracks in the stable structure of our society due to the formation of conflicting factions. Therefore, certainly for many years, we must accept the continuation of an autocratic authority if the introduction of the new male sex is to be effected without organized resistance and opposition. Do you understand the reasoning behind that philosophy?"

"It sounds like computer talk to me," said Koralin. "Anyway, I am not concerned with your forward-planning strategy in that sense. What does concern me is the future and the fate of Alph himself. If he belongs to anybody, he belongs to me."

"He belongs to the world."

"But in what sense? As a kind of machine to pump out your precious gametes in their millions for selective artificial insemination? Why, they do that to cattle."

"Indeed they do—and very efficient and productive it is." A surprising thought occurred suddenly to Davana. "You are not seriously suggesting that we should all wait until the male child reaches late puberty and early adolescence to indulge in crude person-to-person impregnation by"—she hesitated at the word—"*penetration* of the female in the fashion of the lower animals. . . ."

Koralin had no immediate answer to that proposition, so Davana continued. "For one thing. it would be criminally wasteful of gametes. For another, it would introduce into the boy's mind false concepts of his right to select a partner whether she were eugenically cleared or not. It might give him a false sense of power and potential dominance over the female—a contingency that must not be permitted to occur. And, in any case, such a procedure was positively rejected by the mathematical model and the computers."

"I was not thinking in terms of absolutes," Koralin tried to explain, "but rather to combine in some way the impersonal service to society laid down by the computers with an intimate personal relationship with a woman, or certain women, so that the boy, as he grows into a man, will be able to live a life which, as a male, he could regard as normal—at least in part, if not wholly so. Even we, in our Lesbian society, are now permitted to choose our partners on emotional grounds."

"Lesbians do not reproduce from the erotic amusements," Davana pointed out. "The important question of productivity in terms of new life does not enter into the relationship. It is always a sterile liaison. In Project Alpha the objectives are quite different. We are dedicated to produce new male generations in quantity to conform with eugenic specifications. Of course, the growth of the male sex will accelerate swiftly in quantitative terms. It may well be that by the time the second generation emerges it will be possible to relax the procedural regulations so that men may occasionally be permitted to indulge the primitive content of their collective sexual drive—provided an acceptable level of gamete wastage can be tolerated—if that is what you want."

"It is not what I want," Koralin protested. "It is what the boy himself may eventually want."

Davana smiled. "How can he want what he has never known? Life for him will be what it had always been. You cannot describe color to a blind man, and he will adapt—if indeed he needs to adapt. Life for all of us is what it actually is, and not some unguessable might-have-been. So you must be patient Koralin, and concern yourself with your protégé's welfare within the terms of reference of Project Alpha. Otherwise . . ."

She left the sentence unfinished and stood up, still smiling her fixed smile. Koralin knew that the interview was at an end. With despondency in her heart, she thanked her superior and left the office, retiring to her own room to try to resolve the confusion in her mind.

I suppose this is the way any government could be expected to think and plan under the circumstances, Koralin thought. The opaque louvres of the window had been partly closed, casting the room into glooming shadow, so that even the bowl of red and yellow flowers on the small dressing table looked ashen and monochrome.

Optimization—it is a sickening word. Economy of raw material, cost effectiveness, maximum productivity, minimum wastage—all the jargon of computerized accounting. Somewhere, at this very instant, computers would be retrieving the Project 2A files from their databanks, updating them to accommodate the latest developments and amending programs to deal with new contingency situations arising from real events where they differed form the hypothetical mathematical model.

The trouble was that to a computer a human being as such did not exist—it was merely a data-collection input device, comparable with an interactive terminal but capable of carrying out instructions and directives issued by the central processor. Human emotions, liaisons and affinities had to be transcribed into biochemical or psychometric terms. To a computer a color was merely an electromagnetic frequency measured in angstrom units, but it could have no conception of the redness of red, or the blueness of blue. It could tell you with perfect accuracy that the addition of the frequencies of red and green would produce a frequency known as yellow—but without knowing what yellowness, in the subjective sense, was.

And all that the computers knew of Alph as a nine-year-old boy was the stark data defined at length in the Handbook, *Project Alpha—Analyses and Optimization by Variational Parameters.* The same efficient binary arithmetic could be applied just as effectively to the design and construction of a new steel rolling mill or a supersonic jetliner or a nuclear power-grid network. To the computers all things were equal, and none were more equal than others.

Half-heartedly she attempted to analyze her own feelings: I suppose that in truth I am being emotional, and that is a bad thing. It could be dangerous. I shall need to exercise control if I am to be permitted to stay here. I think I may have offended Davana, but she is a wise and resilient woman, and adept at evaluating people's motives. And behind that brusque mask she wears, I suspect there is a kindly heart—but she, too, must observe the rigid protocol of our way of life.

Nevertheless, something must be done if Alph is ever to live the life of a normal human being; otherwise he will merely be a prisoner and enforced donor of gametes until he is of no further use to society, and then he will be discarded as if he were the last man instead of the first.

But for the moment there was nothing she could do,

and there was nothing to be gained by allowing the problem to obsess her conscious mind. Disturbed and restless, she closed her eyes and fell into a light uneasy sleep, where the problem, in the guise of dreams and fantasies, continued to dominate her unconscious mind.

Chapter Eight

As Head of State, Galinia was not noticeably a happy woman, for she was essentially a disciple of change, whereas the functions of her high office demanded the maintenance of stability (and sometimes, she thought, stagnation). Having led the reversionist uprising to its successful revolutionary victory, she had naturally been appointed leader of the people by the people. But to lead a nation in war is one thing; to lead it in peace can be a diabolically different assignment, as many statesmen throughout history have discovered to their disillusionment.

Not that Galinia was disillusioned. She was, if anything, bored. She was weary of non-events that hardly merited the attention of a computer, let alone a human being. She was critical of the efficient fail-safe organization of society and its processes and services. It would make a pleasant change for things to go wrong occasionally—but one had to rely on nature for such favors. An occasional tornado or earthquake, and perhaps a tidal wave or two, tended to break the monotonous routine of a virtually self-administering administration; but even so, such catastrophes were dealt with expeditiously by highly sophisticated emergency routines.

She was a tall handsome woman of rugged bone-structure, possibly in her late forties, with surprisingly protuberant and well-rounded breasts, which was contrary to the generally accepted flat-chested fashion and, it was whispered, was the result of hormone injections. She knew of the whispering but was unperturbed by it. Breasts were one of the anatomical insignia of womanhood, and as leader of a reversionist society that was dedicated to the reintroduction of the male sex, a woman ought logically to look like a woman. The rest of the population would adopt the style in due course.

Perhaps for the same reason she wore her hair longer that was customary, and although it was lacquered, the color was golden, so that apart from the metallic sheen it looked natural enough. Certainly it contrasted strangely with the greens, blues, purples and silvers of the many women with more exotic tastes. Her dress followed the usual style—cape, skirt and sandals. The only indication of her seniority of office was a narrow golden collar bearing an embossed oval seal, which she wore around her neck. The watch on her wrist was of the standard isotope-powered pattern that remained accurate to within one millisecond in a century.

In the early years following the revolution she had traveled a great deal to assist in coordinating international policies, but now she seldom went far. The world was much the same wherever you happened to be, from the polar regions to the equator, and each city was a carbon copy of the next, as though they had all rolled off the same gigantic production line. In any case, global communications were so comprehensive and diverse as to render movement virtually unnecessary. Why travel half-way around the world to talk to a colleague in the Antipodes when one could, with the touch of a button, conjure up a life-size three-dimensional color image of her in one's own office?

Galinia's executive suite was a circular penthouse built in three tiers, like a wedding cake, on top of the Silver Tower in the center of Lon, the capital city. It

was the tallest building in Europe and one of the highest
in the world. The exterior of the skyscraper was clad in
impeccably smooth polished alloy, so that, mirrorlike,
the walls reflected the sky and the clouds and the surrounding urban structure. Because of this, the Silver
Tower often acquired a curious invisibility against its
background, or it took on the mirage-like translucency
of a glass structure, but its black shadow in the sunlight was real enough.

The bottom tier of the three circular executive rooms
contained the secretariat and communications links of
the Head of State. Above, on the second level, was the
conference room, where the Mistresses of government
dealt with matters of day-to-day administration. At the
top, in the smallest of the rooms—which nevertheless
measured more than fifty feet in diameter—Galinia
reigned in comfortable isolation. A continuous window
built into the circular wall afforded a panoramic view
of the city from an altitude of well over a mile above
ground, though frequently the scene was obscured by
low-lying clouds, and one looked out through the glass
into tenuous cotton-wool.

The desk was massive and three-sided, with ample
space for the battery of communication devices, terminals, intercom units and video screens, all within
fingertip reach. Low bookshelves under the window
housed official volumes and documents for immediate
reference, but the mass of State papers and microfilmed
records were stored in a separate library and available
instantly through the secretariat. The entire building was
the seat of government for the country, embracing all
Ministries and Departments, and it extended deep into
the ground, where the giant computers worked inces-
santly, day and night.

There were times when Galinia, who was a practical
woman, felt somewhat idiotic sitting alone in her high-
flying penthouse. It seemed a pointless occupation.
There was work to be done, of course, such as making

sure that other people were doing *their* work, and documents and decrees to sign and seal, and conferences to chair—but seldom a decision to make, for a decision implied options and alternative courses of action, and the machinery of contemporary society ran so smoothly that alternatives seldom if ever arose. Unashamedly, she missed the tactical rough and tumble of the brief revolution, when in the thrust and parry of open conflict vital decisions had to be taken from instant to instant, and where the wrong decision could spell death. And even the civil war itself had been triggered by one swift, sure-minded decision—that of Koralin, a young woman scarcely out of her teenage, whose cool act of incredible courage had changed the very shape and structure of human society.

Courage? Galinia smiled sourly. Probably not. The bravest deeds are done in a sweat of paralyzing fear, as she knew herself from experience. Koralin had probably been quaking in her sandals when she stole the body of the male child from the incubator. Oh, it was courage right enough—the true stubborn courage of the calculated risk taken against the odds, as opposed to the shallow flag-waving heroics and histrionics of popular conception.

When the history of this century comes to be written, thought Galinia, they will name Koralin as the heroine of our times, and myself as the leader of the people. And yet today it is I who gain the recognition, while Koralin lives unseen, unheard and forgotten. But she is not a leader and never will be. The heroine and the leader are two different animals. Nevertheless, Koralin should be recognized—she should have been honored in some way as a reward for her heroic deed.

She thought idly about that for a while and finally decided that it was too late. So many years had elapsed since the event that any kind of retrospective honor would appear to be apologetic and might even be resented by the people. There were, however, other ways of showing appreciation and favor—a soft executive job with a luxury apartment and a generous pension, for example. That could be arranged, if the other woman was agreeable—wherever she might be at this moment.

Galinia fingered a red switch on an intercom unit.

"Where is the Koralin woman?"

"Identity number, Mistress? There are many Koralins."

"Find out. She is the Koralin of the Test 454 incident."

'I'll interrogate the databank."

Silence for a few seconds, then: "Video four."

Green lettering flashed onto one of the monitor screens on the desk. *Koralin Lon/Cyt/RD File AKK 2034419/MF/88724—Present location seconded Al-Pha Project unit in Alphaville.*

"Oh," said Galinia, pressing the button that deleted the message. She should have remembered, of course, for it was she who had personally approved Koralin's co-opted appointment to the Project Alpha Executive Committee against some opposition from the other committee members. Perhaps Koralin had received her reward, after all. At least she could keep a protective eye on the precious male child that could so easily have cost her her life. She dismissed Koralin from her mind.

Coincidentally, at that moment a scrambled priority message was being decoded in the Intelligence Operations Room at a lower level of the Silver Tower. The preamble indicated that the text was of the highest priority and for the personal information of the Head of State only. Thus, when decoded the message was still concealed in a secondary code that could only be transcribed into plain language by Galinia herself, using a special machine installed in her office.

The message was delivered by hand. Galinia opened the sealed envelope and briefly scanned the meaningless groups of letters on the form. She took it to a small

metal cabinet near the wall, operated the dial of a combination lock, and waited for the front to swing open.
On a second combination dial inside the cabinet she
spelled out the first and last letter groups of the message, which formed the decoding indicator of the day,
and then inserted the form into a slot. A few seconds
later a sheet of green paper emerged from another slot.

Quickly she took it and read the text, for the print
would disappear completely and permanently within
half a minute. The instruction was simple enough:
*Project Alpha—Implement Phase 2B forthwith—Da-
vana Alphaville.* Her face showed no reaction, even
though this was the vital message that the various Heads
of State had been waiting for years past.

She returned to the desk and typed out a curt acknowledgment on an official form: *Project Alpha—
Phase 2B implementation begins.* This had to be encoded
in her office and then sent by special messenger to the
Intelligence Operations Room for further encoding and
onward translation to Alphaville, wherever that might
be located.

Galinia found the concept of Alphaville immensely
irritating, not because of the security precautions, which
were no doubt justified, but because of the impenetrable
secrecy concealing the location of the site. True, there
were subversive elements in the new reversionist society,
just as there were in any society; they comprised the
relics of the original autocratic administration and its
supporters, but they were dormant, quiescent and dis-
armed, and certainly powerless to carry out any major
coup, whether aimed at the male child or authority in
general. Alphaville possessed more electronic protection
and camouflage systems than any other restricted urban
zone in the world, in particular, unseen radiation screens
to absorb and deflect probing radar and infrared beams
in such a way that the urban profile of the small township was indistinguishable from its natural environment.
Nor could aerial reconnaissance and photography help,

for above and around Alphaville hung a transparent dome of ionized gass with reflective and refractive properties that produced a visual blending with whatever the surrounding environment might be.

It was all very annoying, partly because it frustrated her instinctive feminine curiosity, but mainly because it implied an undermining of her authority as Head of State. This was particularly so when one considered that the male child had been given the breath of life in a laboratory in her own country, and was rightly one of her own citizens. That the International Alpha Supervisory Council had elected to make the male child the common property of all nations by an almost unanimous vote (only Galinia had abstained) merely exacerbated the situation. Which was, of course, why the international property contained in Alphaville had to be concealed from the nations of the world as a whole.

Now, at least, she could go ahead and set up what might be termed her own "Alpha-2B-ville" in her own country, and that would be national property. Plenty of security and protection, of course, though not on the same scale as Alphaville itself. In fact, the local center already existed in the form of an expanded parthenogenetic birth center, a function for which the buildings above ground level were still used. It was below the ground, descending floor after floor into the earth, that Alpha 2B prenatal quarters and laboratories were installed. At the moment they were empty and waiting, but now the time had come to fill them with scientists and doctors and selected young women who, if all went well, would bear the first token generation of human males, and a new chapter in history would begin. Well, at least things were beginning to move, and one could feel the faint stirring of enthusiasm.

She closed the door of the decoder and locked it. Then she called the secretariat on the intercom. "Internal Ministerial stand-by. There will be a top-level conference of all Senior Mistresses at"—she glanced at her watch—"sixteen hundred precisely. Priority imperative."

That done, she took an abridged version of the official handbook on Phase 2B procedure from the shelf and busied herself in rereading it and making relevant notes.

As a conference, it was short and to the point, for Galinia did not believe in wasting words, nor did she permit others to. In any case, the departmental Mistresses concerned had been previously briefed on the program that was now to be put into effect. Galinia was simply concerned to make sure that the administrative mechanism was ready to go into operation, and that there would be no hitches or errors.

The site for Phase 2B was ready and equipped, and suitably qualified staff had already been short-listed for posting. The final selection could now take place. Special security measures would be put into effect forthwith. The parthenogenetic center above ground would be phased out and closed down over a period of several weeks, so that the entire establishment could be devoted to the secret operation. But the biggest part of the preliminary work fell to two Mistresses—the one responsible for education and training, and the other concerned with applied eugenics.

"Your brief is simple in essence, but may prove difficult in practice," Galinia explained. "From all women in the age-group from eighteen to twenty-five years inclusive, eugenically perfect individuals are to be screened and segregated."

"How perfect?" asked the Mistress of Eugenics, as if there were a degree of perfection.

"In theory, to the specification laid down by Keisintel in her complete three-dimensional DNA model. In practice, that is not yet possible, and the best we have achieved in eugenic selection has approximated to eighty-seven percent of perfection. In the case of Project Alpha an extremely high standard is called for, since the male gametes are random and have a low eugenic selection factor. The minimum acceptable screening factor for females, as laid down in the Handbook, is eighty percent of Keisintel optimum."

"That is extremely high," the Mistress of Eugenics remarked. "It will severely limit the number of candidates."

"Not quite so much as one might imagine," Galinia said. "The statutory age for eugenic tests to determine suitability for parthenogenetic service is twenty-six— that is, after the completion of education and training. For the purposes of Alpha 2B the catchment age group has been set at a much lower level. These younger women have not yet been tested, and because they are younger they will, on a statistical basis, yield a larger proportion of eugenic positives, as our techniques have been refined in recent decades."

The Mistress of Education and Training was showing fidgety signs of concern and disapproval. "Surely this will mean an interruption of the educational program. That would be contrary to statutes."

"It is a question of priorities. Project Alpha is authorized by an international statute which overrides national laws. There will be facilities for study at the Phase 2B center and, of course, an additional year will be added to the educational program of selected candidates for each year spent in the Phase 2B Center, up to the age limit of thirty."

"But it does mean that all recruits will be taken from the undergraduate stratum of our society."

"Quite—and throughout the world. It is the most viable age group for conception and gestation."

"But our *best* undergraduates. I mean, presumably the Keisintel psychometric tests on psychological balance, aptitudes, abstract synthesis, and so on are to be included . . ."

"Of course. Again to a minimum specification of eighty percent of Keisintel's model. You see, nothing but the best will do."

The other woman uttered a dubious grunting sound. "Very well, but it will take time."

"It will take as little time as possible. During the next week or so area Medical Officers and their staffs will visit the universities and colleges to take biopsy samples for preliminary spectroanalysis. We can then prepare a short list of likely candidates for total screening at the official center. We are expected to have the first few suitable females installed and ready for insemination within twenty days. Understood?"

Both Mistresses nodded slowly. Galinia glanced around at the other departmental heads, who had chosen to remain silent, as the matter under discussion did not fall directly within their responsibilities.

"Any questions?"

A pause; then a woman asked: "We understand the priority, but what about the security category?"

"Category 'A' Secret. That means absolute. All communications other than to me, personally, by the spoken word in this office, must be routed through the Intelligence Operations Room. Anything more?"

Silence. Some slight shaking of heads.

"Right. The meeting is concluded. The next step is immediate action."

The women left the office in silence and dispersed to their various departments.

Chapter Nine

During the warm languid summer Lycia and
Crinila spent three weeks together on a leisurely tour of
North Africa and parts of Europe. For Lycia it was
part of the official university recess, and for Crinila, the
remainder of her statutory annual vacation from her job
in the Department of Historical Archives. There was
more to it than just a touring holiday from Lycia's point
of view; it was an idyllic interlude of romantic and
erotic togetherness which was in almost every way
parallel to the archaic custom of the honeymoon. At
any rate, it was the first time she had ever enjoyed a
monopoly of Crinila's body and affection for more than
just a few fleeting hours.

Crinila herself was more circumspect about the relationship. After all, she was an older woman, nearly
twenty-nine years of age, while Lycia was just approaching her nineteenth birthday, and as an albino, though
genetically imperfect, she had never lacked earnest pro-
testations of love and infatuation from countless admirers. Because of this there was, perhaps, a hint of
condescension in her manner, or it may have been no
more than the patronizing air that maturity often lends
to one in the presence of the more naive and inexperienced.

Lycia had in recent years grown extremely beautiful

and well shaped by contemporary standards, and she possessed intelligence of a high order—not simply the sponge-like capacity to learn which could be, and was, measured by devious tests, but a questioning intelligence that pondered the apparent absoluteness of data presented to her by the outside world. This was simply an attitude of mind, with no depth of philosophy to sustain it, though that might come later in life. She was not in any sense a rebel, but rather a conformist who sometimes wondered precisely what she was supposed to conform to, and why.

The erotic play was both an art and a science, as taught at school from an early age. It was a natural, though not necessarily overt, function of the body, which one could exercise alone and in privacy if necessary but was immensely enhanced in the act of reciprocal sharing with another woman—the more so if emotional bonds of affection existed between the partners. In certain communities group erotic play conducted simultaneously between a number of women, sometimes as many as a dozen, was accepted as a sophisticated refinement of the art, but it was more usual for women to pair off, as this created a more exciting sense of mutual intimacy. And, of course, one always discovered, by experiment and sometimes by accident, ecstatic variations which had not been part of the school curriculum.

To Lycia and her sisters of the era this was sex, and the female body had been exquisitely designed, with the utmost streamlined economy, to provide the maximum of delight in the minimum of space. It was a unique nervous reflex that seemed to have no other purpose than to transport one at will into an uncontrollable paroxysm of delicious and delirious orgasm. That the bodily organs concerned with conception, gestation and birth were anatomically adjacent was a matter of coincidence. There was no logical correlation between the one and the other. Orgasm was no more involved in birth than was birth in orgasm.

This point of detail had often exercised Lycia's quizzical mind, because one could not avoid making comparisons with the crude and, to many people, disgusting behavior of the animals of the field. One could not justify any analogy between humans and animals, but there was no denying that the basic biological mechanisms were similar. There seemed to be some doubt as to whether female animals experienced orgasm in any form at all, though it was certain that the males did—orgasm was a subjective experience, so one could never be sure, no could one evaluate it either qualitatively or quantitatively.

It was all very curious. The mechanism for producing orgasm in the male animal (and in the human male, for that matter) was so positioned that it became automatically stimulated in the act of penetrating the female, thereby combining a dual function and undeniably providing an incentive for the male to seek copulation, whether it was aware or not of the simultaneous fertilizing function. Now this was certainly not true of the female. The two functions were quite separate, and, indeed, the cyclic rhythm of female fertility was such that the greater proportion of coitus was wasted in the reproductive sense, with a corresponding wastage of live gametes.

Certain scientists had suggested that sexual behavior in animals was merely a clumsy and primitive approach to what evolution had refined in the human being to a system approaching perfection. The fact that the human male was no longer necessary for perpetuation of the species was in itself evidence that the male had always possessed a built-in obsolescence. Men had been a compromise solution while nature awaited the development of parthenogenesis as the true mode of reproduction.

That made sense, in a way. But if it were true, then

why all the fuss about the male child? Why the reversionist revolution heralding the return of the male sex? Didn't nature know best, after all—at least, better than womankind? And who on earth among women, possessing any culture or sensibility, would wish to be brutally penetrated by the grotesque appendage of some resurrected obsolete creature that should have been allowed to rest undisturbed in its grave?

To Lycia the subject was baffling, but at the same time absorbing in a way she found difficult to define. Crinila seemed to have more understanding of the matter, and occasionally found it amusing, though Lycia never knew why. No doubt it had to do with Crinila's work in compiling and collating historical archives for databank and microfilm recording and supervising the automatic translating machines that processed and transcribed documents and books from the archives of other nations.

The trouble with Crinila was that she never liked to argue or to discuss a subject in any depth. It was not that her thinking was superficial but rather that she considered time too precious to waste in the pursuit of inconclusive and unproductive discussion. At best she would occasionally throw out a hint or two that pointed to veiled knowledge deeper in her mind. Lycia suspected that there were certain security restraints in her professional work that prevented her from mentioning historical aspects of the male sex.

The best time to talk to Crinila was at night, lying in each other's embrace, with sleep gently descending upon tired and satiated bodies and minds.

"Crinila," Lycia had asked on one occasion, "if you were in charge of the male child, what would *you* do with it?"

"How should I know? What would *you* do, Lycia?"

"Well, what if the male child grew up to be a man, as I suppose it will, if it is allowed to—what would you do then?"

"I should pat it on the head and give it a bone to eat."

"But seriously..."

"Lycia, you do ask the strangest questions. The answer to that one is buried somewhere deep inside a computer."

"Would you allow it to play with you?"

Crinila laughed. "To *play* with me? What on earth do you mean by that?"

"You know perfectly well what I mean."

A brief sigh. "If you mean—would I allow it to behave as men behaved five or six hundred years ago, I should think it highly unlikely. But men had their uses. They were strong and hard and militant. They were good at things like heavy engineering and space flight and geological and underwater mining. They were good in research and the sciences, and in the arts, too. One could harness such a creative drive, but it would need to be kept under very tight rein."

Lycia thought about that for a moment. "Do you think they will start to breed men for that purpose— as technological slaves under the control of women?"

"What a wonderful thought," Crinila murmured dreamily.

"I hadn't thought of it that way before," Lycia admitted. "The trouble is that one tends to think of men just in terms of their sex function and forgets all the other things they could be made to do."

"Two-legged beasts of burden," Crinila suggested.

"You are laughing at me again."

Crinila stroked her partner's hair. "Not really, though I'm rather amused by all the fuss you're making about men. Shall I tell you a secret? You and I will probably never even see a real live man in our lifetimes. Even if the male child is fertile, and that is open to doubt, there will be very few males in the world for a long time to come, and they will be slow to generate. And even then eugenic strains will have to be approved

and evolved, and that could take centuries. So, my
lovely Lycia, I think the most we shall ever see of any
real man will be a photograph or an image on a video
screen. The chances of our being 'played with', as you
so tastefully put it, by a crude and brutal male animal
are remote to infinity and beyond."

"Oh," was all that Lycia could find to say. It almost
sounded as if she were disappointed. But Crinila was
right, of course, as she invariably was. The new men
would multiply slowly, hidden away in secret places
where they could be studied and analyzed under strict
control. The first few generations woul be regarded as
gamete-generating prototypes from which, ultimately,
a strain could be bred and stabilized that would meet
the Keisintel eugenic specifications. And in the meantime today's familiar matriarchal society would continue on a business-as-usual basis. Yes, come to think
of it, she *was* disappointed. Not that she had any desire
to be mauled by a real man, or even approach within
touching distance of one, but because somewhere deep
in her mind was the hope that an era of rapid change
was imminent—that a new and different kind of society was about to be born, and that life would be won-
derfully and miraculously transformed. But it was only
the hope of a prisoner impatiently pacing his cell while
awaiting the moment of release.

"Well, who wants men, anyway?" she said with an
attempt at nonchalance that didn't quite come off.

Crinila smiled in the darkness. "Why, nobody, Lycia
darling. Not even the men themselves will want men.
All they will ever want is women."

At the end of the vacation Lycia returned reluctantly
to the university to find that all students had to under-
go a detailed medical and psychological test and supply a generous quota of biopsy samples. No explanation was given for this unusual procedure. Medical
check-ups were common enough, but not in such metic-

ulous detail by such a large imported squad of clinical staff, and the biopsy tests were generally associated with genetic analysis and eugenic selection. Naturally, all this gave rise to a great deal of speculation among the students.

"It's exactly the kind of thing they do when you are twenty-six," said one. "Selection for parthenogenetic duty."

"But we are far too young," protested another.

"Perhaps the law has been changed. We are not too young biologically."

"But it would interfere with our education. . . ."

"Anyway, if the law had been changed we should have heard about it. I don't like all the secrecy. Why couldn't they say what it was for?"

"It just goes to show that it can't be connected with parthenogenesis. There's nothing secret about *that!*"

Lycia said: "Nevertheless, it was typical of a preliminary eugenic test. It could be connected with the male child."

Astonished silence for a few moments. "The male child? But how?"

"The male child is still a baby."

"No," said Lycia. "The male child is—let me see, about nine or ten years old."

"Well, that is almost a baby."

"It is also almost an adult in a biological sense. Perhaps they want to do some genetic experiments."

"Not on us, surely?"

"Why not?"

"It would be—well, it would be against the law."

"No. Outside the law, perhaps, but not against it. The law applies to parthenogenesis. This would be different."

"You seem to know a lot about it, Lycia. What else do you know?"

"I know nothing at all," said Lycia. "It's all guesswork. But if you can think of a better explanation. . ."

They couldn't, and Lycia was left with the feeling that they suspected her of possessing secret information, and that they didn't quite trust her—which was a very unpleasant feeling for a young woman whose thinking tended to be naive rather than devious. It was probably her conversations with Crinila that had inspired the reference to the male child, and anyway, it was all speculation. But there was one thing they could be certain about—something big and important was afoot, and whatever was going to happen would not take long in the happening.

This impression was confirmed the following day when it was learned that similar medical examinations and biopsy tests had been carried out in other universities, not only in Europe but throughout the world. Bad news travels fast in a world of rapid communications, and one could hardly interpret global vetting on such a scale as good news. Rumors spread like a bush fire, from an attack of spontaneous sterility that would wipe out the female sex, just as it had erased men, to a lethal virus epidemic originating in the Far East (why did it always have to be the Far East?) that would decimate the human race. And there were rumors concerning the male child, too, but for some reason few people seemed to take them very seriously, perhaps because sterility and plague offered more sensational talking points.

In due course authority became aware of the rumors and dealt with them coolly and efficiently by arranging for a brief notice to be displayed on university notice boards. It stated: *The recent series of medical examinations was part of an international statistical survey commissioned by Central Administration for long-range planning purposes, and may be repeated from time to time as necessary.* That was all. It was true in essence but said nothing in effect. It damped down the overtones of hysteria and allayed anxiety, but left the question posed.

she had to catch the ear and undivided
Davana, the chairman of the Central Exec-
mittee, but that was no easy task, for Da-
were tightly scheduled. To make matters
ana's secretary was an arrogant and sarcastic
an of oriental caste, who had obviously
ed to act as an impassable barrier rather
neans of reasonable access to her mistress.
ck of official status in the scientific com-
d as a kind of inverse priority factor.

eks went by before, one morning, she acci-
countered Davana in a deserted corridor
the document and file registry. The other
s carrying a large bundle of papers under
nd seemed in a hurry. Koralin stopped and
od to one side, wondering fearfully whether
isk speaking: and, indeed, Davana had al-
ed her without acknowledgment when, partly
tense surprise, she said:

cuse me, Mistress Davana ..."
er woman halted in her tracks and slowly
und. Suddenly there was recognition in her
it occurred to Koralin that she hadn't even
r at all until that moment. Her thoughts had
een far, far away.

norning, Koralin. Do you wish to say some-

I would like to talk to you about many
are troubling me."
extremely busy at this moment. Central Ad-
n is calling for program amendments."
ur convenience, Mistress—when you have a
to spare."
re for what? I am never free for more than
nutes at unpredictable times. Have a word
ecretary. Perhaps she can find a vacant slot
table."

Five days later Lycia was summoned to the office of
the university Registrar, who handed her a sealed envelope marked *Private*. "Do not open it yet," said the
Registrar. "You are to go away for a week or two for
further medical tests at a special center."

Noting Lycia's change of expression, she smiled and
added: "No cause for alarm. There is nothing wrong
with you. It is part of a very important research project which may not, in the end, concern you at all. You
will be well looked after."

"When do I go?" asked Lycia.

"Now. Collect any personal possessions you may
wish to take with you, but don't take clothing and
toilet articles. They will be supplied. When you have
packed and left the university grounds, but not before, you may open the envelope and go to the address you will find contained inside. It is an address
in Lon, not very far from here. There you will doubtless meet other students who will be accompanying
you on this assignment."

"And my friends here—will they ...?"

The Registrar shook her head. "You are the only
student selected from this university—at present, that
is—though there may be more later. So you see, you
are highly privileged. I can assure you that the standards they have set are extremely high."

"Will I be coming back here—after the tests?"

"We must wait and see," said the Registrar in a
kindly voice. "I suppose it depends on you and the
government. I am only an intermediary—a passer-on of
messages, as it were. But I am sure that everything
will be for your benefit and welfare. We shall naturally
keep your residential quarters available pending further instructions."

With that somber reassurance echoing in her mind,
Lycia left the Registrar's office and went to her private
room to pack. Her movements were slow and automatic, her brain torpid. Somehow thinking was not

called for. It was a characteristic of any governmental measure; it tended to be so absolute that thought could not help. One was, as it were, a pawn moved willy-nilly on an unseen chessboard, and even if a pawn could think, why should it bother to?

She did exactly as instructed, packing a small case with a few personal items, including her diary, pocket tape recorder, and a three-dimensional color photograph of Crinila. For a wild moment she thought she would telephone Crinila to let her know what was happening, but some inner caution warned her against it. Later, perhaps, there would be an opportunity. For the moment it was wiser to obey orders, unthinkingly, like a robot.

Presently, with a gloomy sense of finality and foreboding, she left the campus and opened the sealed envelope. Inside was a card with an address printed on it. She knew the building quite well—it was a medical center and transit station for parthenogenetic candidates, and was within walking distance. With an increasing sense of unreality she walked slowly toward whatever the unguessable future held in store for her.

Chapte

Certain aspects of the Pro
a matter of growing concern
the treatment of Alph himsel
attitude of the scientists respo
standable; they were imperso
an equally impersonal experi
was merely a passive and unv
was little or no communicat
others, it was because they
not exactly regard her as an
redundant deadwood prone to
sulting from ignorance of the
project.

True, she had access to the
they were extremely advanced
stand and interpret for one
had been confined to the na
microcytology. The mathemati
complex, and most of the pres
fined in the esoteric program l
ters, with which she was only
case, her discontent did not
computer language; it could be
quite unsophisticated words.

Someho
attention o
utive Com
vana's day
worse, Da
young wo
been sele
than as a
Koralin's
munity ac

Many
dentally
leading t
woman v
one arm
politely s
she dare
ready pa
to her ov
"Oh, e
The o
turned a
eyes, an
noticed
probably
"Good
thing?"
"Pleas
things th
"I am
ministra
"At y
little tir
"To
a few
with my
in my t

Five days later Lycia was summoned to the office of the university Registrar, who handed her a sealed envelope marked *Private*. "Do not open it yet," said the Registrar. "You are to go away for a week or two for further medical tests at a special center."

Noting Lycia's change of expression, she smiled and added: "No cause for alarm. There is nothing wrong with you. It is part of a very important research project which may not, in the end, concern you at all. You will be well looked after."

"When do I go?" asked Lycia.

"Now. Collect any personal possessions you may wish to take with you, but don't take clothing and toilet articles. They will be supplied. When you have packed and left the university grounds, but not before, you may open the envelope and go to the address you will find contained inside. It is an address in Lon, not very far from here. There you will doubtless meet other students who will be accompanying you on this assignment."

"And my friends here—will they...?"

The Registrar shook her head. "You are the only student selected from this university—at present, that is—though there may be more later. So you see, you are highly privileged. I can assure you that the standards they have set are extremely high."

"Will I be coming back here—after the tests?"

"We must wait and see," said the Registrar in a kindly voice. "I suppose it depends on you and the government. I am only an intermediary—a passer-on of messages, as it were. But I am sure that everything will be for your benefit and welfare. We shall naturally keep your residential quarters available pending further instructions."

With that somber reassurance echoing in her mind, Lycia left the Registrar's office and went to her private room to pack. Her movements were slow and automatic, her brain torpid. Somehow thinking was not called for. It was a characteristic of any governmental measure; it tended to be so absolute that thought could not help. One was, as it were, a pawn moved willy-nilly on an unseen chessboard, and even if a pawn could think, why should it bother to?

She did exactly as instructed, packing a small case with a few personal items, including her diary, pocket tape recorder, and a three-dimensional color photograph of Crinila. For a wild moment she thought she would telephone Crinila to let her know what was happening, but some inner caution warned her against it. Later, perhaps, there would be an opportunity. For the moment it was wiser to obey orders, unthinkingly, like a robot.

Presently, with a gloomy sense of finality and foreboding, she left the campus and opened the sealed envelope. Inside was a card with an address printed on it. She knew the building quite well—it was a medical center and transit station for parthenogenetic candidates, and was within walking distance. With an increasing sense of unreality she walked slowly toward whatever the unguessable future held in store for her.

Chapter Ten

Certain aspects of the Project Alpha program were a matter of growing concern to Koralin—in particular, the treatment of Alph himself. The detached, objective attitude of the scientists responsible for him was understandable; they were impersonal machines conducting an equally impersonal experiment in which she herself was merely a passive and unwelcome observer. If there was little or no communication between her and the others, it was because they discouraged it. They did not exactly regard her as an intruder, but rather as redundant deadwood prone to emotional reactions resulting from ignorance of the proper objectives of the project.

True, she had access to the various handbooks, but they were extremely advanced and difficult to understand and interpret for one whose technical training had been confined to the narrow specialized field of microcytology. The mathematical sections were highly complex, and most of the prescribed routines were defined in the esoteric program languages of the computers, with which she was only vaguely familiar. In any case, her discontent did not require mathematics or computer language; it could be expressed in simple and quite unsophisticated words.

Somehow she had to catch the ear and undivided attention of Davana, the chairman of the Central Executive Committee, but that was no easy task, for Davana's days were tightly scheduled. To make matters worse, Davana's secretary was an arrogant and sarcastic young woman of oriental caste, who had obviously been selected to act as an impassable barrier rather than as a means of reasonable access to her mistress. Koralin's lack of official status in the scientific community acted as a kind of inverse priority factor.

Many weeks went by before, one morning, she accidentally encountered Davana in a deserted corridor leading to the document and file registry. The other woman was carrying a large bundle of papers under one arm and seemed in a hurry. Koralin stopped and politely stood to one side, wondering fearfully whether she dare risk speaking: and, indeed, Davana had already passed her without acknowledgment when, partly to her own tense surprise, she said:

"Oh, excuse me, Mistress Davana ..."

The other woman halted in her tracks and slowly turned around. Suddenly there was recognition in her eyes, and it occurred to Koralin that she hadn't even noticed her at all until that moment. Her thoughts had probably been far, far away.

"Good morning, Koralin. Do you wish to say something?"

"Please. I would like to talk to you about many things that are troubling me."

"I am extremely busy at this moment. Central Administration is calling for program amendments."

"At your convenience, Mistress—when you have a little time to spare."

"To spare for what? I am never free for more than a few minutes at unpredictable times. Have a word with my secretary. Perhaps she can find a vacant slot in my timetable."

"I have already tried, Mistress, and your secretary has never been able to help."

"Well, there you are," said Davana with an air of triumph. "She knows my commitments better than I do. What is it you wish to talk about?"

"The male child."

"Mm..." A frown and a pause. "List your points and have them added to the agenda for the next committee meeting under 'any other business.' My secretary will attend to it."

"This is not a committee matter," Koralin insisted. "I need to talk to you personally as one human being to another."

Surprise flickered momentarily behind Davana's cool grey eyes, as if she considered it an odd concept that people should actually think of each other as human beings.

"You mean—it is something personal?"

"It is about personal things rather than about applied science."

"Oh, very well. I can't stand here arguing indefinitely. I'll see you in my private room tonight just before retiring. Five minutes to midnight. No later."

"Thank you, Mistress. I'll be there."

Davana resumed her stately course as though the interruption had never happened, while Koralin simply stared blankly at her receding back. Well, well, she thought—privilege indeed! To be invited to Davana's private room. Why, it was almost like being received in the privileged guest room of the Head of State. For an instant she shuddered at the thought of her own effrontery and persistence. Whatever must Davana have thought of her? At least the woman had been sufficiently swayed to permit an unwitnessed and unmonitored interview in her own personal suite, though one could never be absolutely sure of privacy—cameras and microphones lurked in the most unlikely places. Still, she didn't care.

Then she smiled sardonically as she tried to visualize the secretary's indignation and anger when and if she learned about the informally arranged meeting. It just wasn't done—not in Alphaville. It was contrary to every rule in the book, and a few more besides. And it all went to prove that beneath Davana's somewhat forbidding and generally unyielding exterior was a heart that had managed to retain a beat or two of common humanity. Which meant that possibly, but only possibly, her views about Alph might receive a sympathetic hearing.

She continued walking along the corridor toward the document registry, only to realize that in the stress of the meeting with Davana she had completely forgotten why she had wanted to go there in the first place. Presumably to refer to some file or other, but the subject had now completely escaped her. Never mind—it couldn't have been all that important. The vital thing was the meeting with Davana—the incredibly won concession allowing her to put her views and feelings to her superior informally and off the record. Far better to concentrate on that for the rest of the day.

She returned to her own room and decided to be systematic about the venture: to think carefully about what she wanted to say and make notes, omitting no important details, and then from the notes compile a list—her own personal agenda—of talking points, as few and concise as possible, but strictly to the point, so as not to waste Davana's valuable time. Such a written guideline was essential, for an opportunity of this kind might never occur again. Davana was too busy to cover the same ground more than once.

She took a piece of paper and wrote at the top *Alph*. At least it was a start. And then she began thinking.

Davana was presumably ready for bed, for she was wearing a long informal dressing gown of thin green material that covered like a drape from neck to toes.

Beneath that she would be naked, as was the habit
of the day. Her room was no less austere and functional than others, though larger and more crammed
with books and papers. A bench in one corner, near
the horizontal window, was fitted with communications equipment of various types, including the inevitable video terminal with its six-band keyboard, which
would be connected directly to a satellite computer.
Sliding doors in facing walls gave access to bathroom
and bedroom. Apart from catering facilities (which
were centralized) it was a self-contained flat of generous size.

In the center of the floor was a round table of metal
and plastic, and against one wall the inevitable desk
with its own adjustable working light. Davana was sitting at the desk, writing on what appeared to be a
printed questionnaire, as Koralin went in. She closed
the door behind her and stood politely by it until the
other woman deigned to notice her presence. Davana
did not keep her waiting long. She abandoned the questionnaire and spun round in her chair.

"Sit down, Koralin, and say what you have to say.
I can give you five minutes."

Koralin's hand, in the pocket of her skirt, was clutching the small piece of paper on which she had written
her carefully prepared "talking points"; but now that
the crucial moment had arrived she found herself unable to produce it, for no good reason that she could
define—other than that it might suggest deliberation
or even premeditated insubordination. Better to wait
and see. Five minutes would hardly be long enough
to cover more than one or two points, anyway.

She sat tensed and upright on a metal-tube chair,
one hand still in her pocket, the other resting limply
on her knee.

"Alph—that is, the male child—is now nearly ten
years old. He appears to be intelligent and perceptive.
He is quick to learn. He has a natural curiosity that

one might expect in a child of his age, but he is not being educated."

Davana's eyebrows moved fractionally in challenge. "He has been taught to communicate," she stated. "He can read and write and has a certain facility with elementary mathematics and a flair for creative handicraft. Is that not enough?"

"At his age," Koralin said, "girls are already at an advanced pre-university level. They have three or four languages, advanced mathematics, and are specializing in various sciences according to their aptitudes. Compared with them, Alph is effectively a moron, through no fault of his own."

"Ah, I see," Davana breathed, as though a great light of understanding had dawned. "You mean he has not received the usual intensive training for university entrance. The answer is very simple—he will not be going to a university, so there is no point in filling his brain with information that he will never need to use."

"But if he is ever to fulfill a useful role in our highly technological society . . ."

"He is doing that already—even at his tender age. He is our only source of male gametes, and he does not require a higher education to perform that function."

"But later in his life, when he is a man—what then?"

Davana frowned with one eye—a curious trick which Koralin was never able to perform herself. "I do not quite understand your question. What then what?—if I may put it that way."

"When he has served his immediate biological purpose here at Alphaville, and the first generation of new males is producing more and more gametes in all the participating countries of the world. What then? He will be twenty, and perhaps older, but still uneducated to take his place in the outside world."

Davana uttered a terse laugh. "Surely you do not seriously imagine that Alph, as you call him, could ever be released from Alphaville as the only male in a world of more than one thousand million females. He would be a freak—a circus animal with urges and instincts totally alien to our culture. Even worse, unless he were first sterilized he could easily jeopardize the entire program of selective eugenic breeding as laid down by Dr. Keisintel. I will go further and predict that not one of the first four or five generations of new males will be permitted to enter our female society as citizens—which takes the matter beyond my lifetime and yours. They will first have to be made eugenically acceptable in sufficient numbers to ensure an adequate balance of sexes for the purpose of controlled natural propagation, and that does not mean one man for every woman. As you are well aware, one man can fertilize many women. Does that answer your question about 'what then'?"

"No," Koralin said, feeling rather disorientated by Davana's crystal-gazing, "unless you are saying that Alph is to be held prisoner in Alphaville for the rest of his life, like a scientific specimen under a microscope."

"You are overdramatizing in an emotional way, Koralin. Project Alpha is an experiment, and like all experiments it must be controlled. The experiment does not end with Alph—it *begins* with him and will continue for generations, but always under control. Do you understand?"

Koralin nodded. She was beginning to understand.

"Look at it from Alph's point of view," Davana went on. "He will remain in a familiar environment, which to him will represent security. This is his world. To take him out of it, even now, could be psychologically damaging. Why, he does not even know he is a male, or that we are females, or what it means. He knows nothing of the female body, but he is already showing a precocious interest in his own. That in itself is producing problems. Although we extract our gamete samples in a clinical way using specially designed equipment and the natural erotic reflexes, he finds the process pleasurable—so much so that we have observed him occasionally resorting to masturbation of a primitive kind, which is undesirable, of course."

"Why? If that is an offense, then all females are equally guilty."

"Females in their auto-eroticism do not shed and waste gametes," Davana explained with a show of patience. "Alph does. The program does not allow for such wastage. It is a point that was not fully explored in the mathematical model, and we are dealing with it. It may be that minor surgery or an inhibiting drug may be necessary, though naturally we do not wish to introduce artificial factors that may distort the overall study and produce spurious conclusions."

She glanced quickly at her watch. "You have had much longer than your allotted time, and I have mentioned confidential matters to put your mind at ease. Be assured that Alph will be well cared for and will have a life of idle contentment that many of us might well envy. And his sons and grandsons will in due course be equally sheltered and privileged. Then one day, in perhaps a century or two, when the genetic and eugenic scientists have completed their task, the new men will be ready to take their rightful place in the world of women, and we shall have achieved a truly reversionist society without disruption, conflict or neurosis."

Davana stood up. "And now, if you will excuse me . . ."

"Thank you, Mistress Davana," said Koralin, moving towards the door. "There is more I would like to say, but it is late and you have been very kind to give me so much of your time. Perhaps some time we could continue . . ."

"We shall see. Just think about what I have already told you. Think carefully, and the logic will become

only too apparent. Above all, avoid emotion and sentiment. We live in an age of reason—not of whimsy.
Goodnight."

"Goodnight," Koralin said as she left the room.

Koralin found it difficult to sleep that night. Her
mind seemed to turn and spin with a spontaneous animation of its own, going over Davana's cool, rational
statements and explanations and trying to pursue the
ramifications in human terms—in Alph's terms. Davana
and thousands of eminent scientists, supported by powerful computers, had to be right—only a fool could
think otherwise. Nothing that Davana had said could
be faulted. A lone Alph set loose in a world of Lesbian
women was impractical, and a lone sterilized Alph set
loose was ludicrous. And it was true that his cytological
DNA structure did not meet the stringent requirements
of the Keisintel specifications, nor would those of many
succeeding male generations. One had to accept that
Keisintel was right. At least, the rest of the world did.

But to visualize Alph growing up and living out his
life in the invisible, isolated fortress of Alphaville,
knowing nothing of the wider environment and accept-
ing everything done to him as normal, was unthinkable
—though not to Davana and her colleagues. That was
a worrying point. It could be that she, Koralin, was
unbalanced, in the grip of some twisted obsession that
prevented her from thinking rationally, or, as Davana
had warned, unable to control some atavistic emotional
element in her nature. That had been true from the
start. It had been emotion and sentiment that had
compelled her to kidnap Test 454 nearly ten years ago,
and not logic and reason, and she had always been
aware of a strong affinity for the child ever since. Of
one thing she was sure: She had not risked her life in

kidnapping Alph for the kind of future that Davana had outlined. But there was nothing she could do about it, and Davana was right.

Or was she? Always that defiant doubt returned to trouble her peace of mind. By what criterion was Davana right? What was expedient for society as a whole could well be neither right nor wrong, and authoritarian approval did not necessarily confer the cachet of a godlike blessing. Human standards were arbitrary standards and could never be absolute. And as for the computers, those so-called decision-making tools, they were merely the processors and echoers of human thinking.

But even if Davana and her colleagues were not right, they possessed the power and the mandate to regard dissenters as wrong, and to deal with them accordingly. What was the point of being right if, as a minority of one, you couldn't possibly win? The sensible thing to do was to accept the verdict of the majority and hold it to be right, even if you thought otherwise. And, even more important, to be discreet and keep your thoughts to yourself if you wished to enjoy the privileges of a free citizen. That was expediency. Back to the beginning—back to Alpha, and Alph.

She turned over in bed and tried to erase the turbulent thought from her mind, for gnawing at an insoluble problem could achieve absolutely nothing. Perhaps what she needed was a lover—the intimate attentions of another woman to anchor her senses and sensibilities in the reality of now, to provide an emotional focus remote from the child, who, if you considered him in cold blood, was essentially a synthetically created freak. But that was wishful thinking, and had been for more years than she cared to recall. If she had failed to form a romantic liaison with another woman in Alphaville, it was because she was an outsider—neither management nor shop floor, as it were. Mainly, she was associated with the Executive Committee, but she was not one of them, nor was she one of the other women at implementation level carrying out the program ordained by the committee. She belonged to no established group, and therefore she belonged to nobody—except perhaps to Alph himself, and that was nothing more than an innocent self-deception.

I must widen my interests, she told herself, her eyes now open and staring into the blackness. It might even be best if I were to go back to Lon, to the normal outside world, for a while—even for a few years. There is nothing I can usefully do here in Alphaville except observe and disapprove and criticize—and worry myself into insomnia and perhaps mental illness.

She closed her eyes again. This time sleep seemed measurably nearer to her fatigued brain. Tomorrow she would see the medico and get some drugs to deal with the insomnia. Clear thinking was called for, and that could not be accomplished in a state of enervation and listlessness. Nor could decision making. And there was no hurry. The days would pass slowly, one by one, just as the years had slipped by, almost unnoticed. Tomorrow the medico. That, at least, was action of a kind, or the promise of action, and its effect was soothing.

Presently she fell asleep, but awoke again before dawn feeling tired and irritable. Although she did not fully realize it, Koralin was under stress, aggravated by the frustration of helplessness. Therefore she was becoming unstable, and a danger to the coldly balanced community in which she was permitted to exist.

Chapter Eleven

Nine months in Partho-8 had seemed like a prison sentence at one time, but in retrospect Lycia could only wonder at her early fears and laugh at her naiveté. It was a great life, rather like living in a luxury hotel with every service and amenity. There were, of course, the boring clinical sessions and the tuition periods, but the latter were more in the nature of a sustaining series of refresher courses rather than intense academic cramming, and nobody seemed to take them very seriously anyway.

She was one of twenty young women at Partho-8—the first carefully selected batch for the Alpha 2B experiment, and therefore, one presumed, the twenty most eugenically perfect females of that age group in the land. At the outset Lycia had found it disconcerting to be surrounded by such exquisite beauty and intelligence, until gradually it dawned on her that she too was one of the chosen, and equally beautiful and intelligent—if one could trust Keisintel's equations. As could be expected in a group conforming to rigid specifications, the women were remarkably alike, particularly beneath the cosmetics and lacquers and sprays, as though impressed with a common stamp of sisterhood; but there were delicate variations in the color of hair and eyes, and to some extent bone structure, within tolerance limits which did not affect the approved eugenic formula. Personalities and temperaments differed too, but not so noticeably that specific types of character were immediately discernible.

Partho-8 was the converted parthenogenetic center, located some fifty miles north of Lon, that had been adopted as the national Alpha-2B-ville, so to speak. Security existed, but it fell well short of the invisibility screening and anonymity of the original Alphaville. Viable male gametes had now been distributed throughout the world, and the chances of politically motivated destruction and sabotage were correspondingly slighter. But the area was nevertheless a restricted zone, and the staff as well as the inmates were confined to the premises and the immediate parkland environment—which was pleasant enough.

The first few days for Lycia had been strange and somewhat trying, despite the obviously high standards of accommodation. The parallel to a luxury hotel was apt enough, for one had the same feeling of transient impermanence—that in a day or so one would be off again to a new destination and more workaday living quarters. All the new arrivals were strangers and pioneers; there were no "old hands" around to tell lurid stories of what was to happen, and the permanent staff made no pronouncements and issued no instructions. It was a settling-in period.

Lycia's room was large and airy, with a curved window overlooking an oval lake in a formal garden. Beyond was the fresh green of meadows and trees. All the apartments were above ground in what had formerly been the entire parthenogenetic center, and the functional prenatal and medical departments and laboratories occupied several levels below ground. Each apartment was fitted with color video and intercom units, and everything was new, from soft carpets to luminous ceilings. The dining room—waitress service and none of that "serve yourself" nonsense—would have done credit to a top-rating Lon hotel. Other amenities included a heated swimming pool and a well-equipped gymnasium, for exercise rated highly in the prenatal program.

Nearly a week elapsed before a formal announcement was made to the selected candidates. By that time they had become adequately acquainted, and the group had begun to break up into the inevitable cluster of cliques in which particular girls seemed to find an affinity in each other, although at this early stage no emotional attachments had crystallized. One morning they were summoned to a small assembly hall. On a dais at one end stood a very distinguished-looking woman draped in a silver cape. Her voice when she spoke was metallic and crisply articulated.

"Welcome to our Partho-8 center, which in my view is the most advanced and sophisticated establishment of its kind in the world," she said. "But first, allow me to introduce myself. I am Dr. Karnax—an unusual name, but one which you will easily remember—and I am in charge of the schedule of work that has been allocated to this center. No doubt most of you have already guessed the true nature of that work. It has to do with Project Alpha, and that, as you know from your university training, is a vital first step in our Reversionist government's long-term plan to reintroduce the male sex into human society. You, as specially chosen daughters of the State, have been elected for the honor of bearing the first generation of male humans to be born in this world for more than five centuries.

"You have been chosen for your extremely high genetic and eugenic qualifications. You are, each of you, living proof of the validity of the biomathematical work to which Dr. Keisintel devoted her entire professional life. The selection process will continue, of course, and others will follow you in this great scientific adventure, but you young women, as you sit listening to me now, are already being recorded in history as the pioneers of what will be without doubt the greatest feat of human engineering of all time.

"Each of you will have a personal medico throughout be responsible for your care and health throughout the experiment, from beginning to end. For the rest, communal activities, exercise and recreation will be supervised by a small but highly trained team, which will include two of the country's most distinguished psychiatrists. No effort or expense will be spared to make sure that your stay here at Partho-8 will be as comfortable as possible, and productive"—she smiled —"in every sense of the word."

Dr. Karnax paused for a moment while she referred to a tiny card which she produced from the pocket of her skirt. Subdued whispering broke out among the girls. Lycia's neighbor said, close to her ear: "She seems a very kindly woman, but you never can tell, can you?" Lycia merely nodded. A face value was merely a face value.

"Now, as to the actual schedule itself," Dr. Karnax continued, "the day-to-day programming will be phsyiological and psychological indications. Obviously professional judgment and flexibility has to be exercised, though I doubt if there will be any significant variation from the predicted standards.

"But in general terms, what will happen is this. We have received here, at the center, a carefully selected sample of live gametes derived from the male child at at the Project Alpha center. They are male-producing gametes, filtered and tested by a very advanced new process. As each of you reaches the correct phase in the estrous cycle—and, of course, that will occur at different times throughout the next month—you will be artificially inseminated and fertilized by these gametes. The operation is simple and in no way uncomfortable.

"The rest follows biologically and automatically. The customary methods of accelerating gestation and inducing birth will not be used—at least, not in the initial series of experiments. Our purpose is to study the development of the natural and unaided embryo and foetus of male sex that has not been produced by parthenogenetic techniques. That is something, I may add, which we have not been able to do for five hundred years or more, outside of animals.

"The process will therefore take about nine months instead of the more usual five or six months in accelerated parthenogenesis. When birth has been achieved, you will be granted a convalescent vacation of six weeks, and then, after further medical tests, you will return to your universities to continue your studies.

"You may, however, be called upon again after an interval of perhaps a year to produce a second male infant. Obviously, the number of young women possessing the extremely high eugenic standards required is necessarily limited. It is unlikely, however, that you will be recruited more than twice for the Project Alpha function."

She paused, then added: "And, by way of compensation, you will be permanently exempted from the normal parthenogenetic propagation duties, which you would be normally expected to undertake from the age of twenty-six onwards—unless, of course, you voluntarily opt for such duties. And, now—are there any questions, bearing in mind that your own medicos will give you all the biological information you may need?"

Silence for quite a long time. At such a moment the first question—the ice-breaker—is always the most difficult to pose. Then somebody asked: "What will happen to the male babies after birth?"

Dr. Karnax said, almost nonchalantly, "Oh, as in the case of parthenogenetic progeny, they will be removed to a State nursery environment."

"Shall we be allowed to see them?"

"Yes, during the short period following birth. The usual procedure will be followed."

"Dr. Karnax," said another student, "can we be sure that these male creatures will meet Keisintel's eugenic standards?"

Dr. Karnax smiled a little patronizingly. "If they don't it will not be your fault." Then, solemn once more: "Clearly they must be substandard, since the Alpha gametes themselves are substandard. However, the first generation of males will provide a basic stock for eugenic selection and breeding along Keisintel's principles. As you can imagine, it will take a long time and many generations of males to achieve results, but the process has to start somewhere, and it starts here, in Partho-8, with you."

Another interval of silence, and then a timid question: "Dr. Karnax, we all know how the beasts of the field behave. Surely we shall not be submitted to such indignities. . . ."

A titter of suppressed laughter rippled through the assembly. Dr. Karnax's manner remained serious, however. "The question of male-female interrelationships is so remote as to be academic, and it is unlikely to be answered in your lifetime. So the small matter of indignity will not arise. The existing techniques of parthenogenesis and the new method of artificial insemination will continue for an indefinite period. The male generations in that context will be regarded as donors for selective eugenic breeding.

"As to what will happen when the scientists have finally produced a generation of Keisintel-approved males—well, that is a matter for conjecture. No doubt the scientists, computers, and politicians of that far distant day will have decided how best to integrate men into human society long before the contingency arises. But it need not concern us. We start the process— they will finish it."

A quick glance around the silent audience. "If there are no further questions . . ." There weren't. "Good. I should like you to assemble here tomorrow morning at nine hundred, when you will meet your respective medicos, and at that point the program will officially start. One final point: While you are resident here at Partho-8, no communication with friends and colleagues in the outside world will be permitted, other than by the written word on special forms available from Administration. Incoming communications are subject to the same embargo. While I personally disapprove of restrictive censorship of this nature, I'm afraid it is required by law, as Project Alpha has a high security rating. However, I am sure that this will not present any great hardship over such a limited period of months."

And that was all. The assembly dispersed, informed up to a point, and slightly bemused, to idle away the hours until the following morning, when the serious business was scheduled to begin.

To Crinila, the sudden disappearance of Lycia was only a temporary loss, for as an albino she had many admirers only too eager to fill any emotional gap in her life. In due course, brief and relatively uncommunicative notes began to arrive from Lycia via the government internal mail service, but they made it clear enough that she had been selected to take part in a special project at a State parthenogenetic center. Crinila needed no further information. Although her interest in the male child had always been rather academic and not without an element of scepticism, she now knew that behind the scenes, without publicity, success of some kind had been achieved—that the male child was not only still alive but was already producing seed, and that the seed was genetically viable enough to justify fertilization tests on young eugenically cleared women.

Her reaction to this realization was twofold. First,

there was a transient feeling of hurt that Lycia should have been classified as eugenically near perfect while she, Crinila, was a genetic outcast through no fault of her own. It was one of the unkind and unfair accidents of life that no society had the right to penalize.

Second, from her day-to-day work in the Department of Historical Archives Crinila had learned a great deal about the old dead world of men, and about man himself as a male animal—his shape, function and activities. Until now, such information had possessed no intrinsic reality; it was part of a mythology which, though fascinating in many respects, one felt had never really happened. But that was no longer so.

Crinila's thinking began to take on what she considered to be a morbid tone. She found her mind focusing more and more obsessively on the male sex, partly, she suspected, because what she had once dismissed so lightly as a kind of fantasy seemed about to materialize in all its chilling imminence. But why chilling? It was surely the word that the vast majority of women would have used, and yet there had been a time when men had not been so regarded. She was logical enough to recognize that the change was one of psychological and emotional attitudes deliberately inculcated by authority in the interests of social survival—the mental and moral support-system for a homosexual culture. Like the rest of humanity, she was ensnared, but because she was already different from the others she often found that she could think differently, too, and question many practices that the rest took for granted.

Added to which she was privileged, because of the nature of her professional work, in having access to information from all over the world that was denied to others: ancient books, pictures, photographs and drawings of an esoteric nature, many of which would be regarded by the Lesbian women of her day as perverted and disgusting because they dealt with male-female conjugation. Her own inbred distaste had slowly dispersed as her reading and studies intensified, just as a medico becomes desensitized through familiarity with suffering and death—though the analogy was not quite accurate.

Sex had been a reality in its heterosexual form, and it was no less urgently demanding today in its homosexual version. The fundamental drive was unchanged, but its mode of fulfilment had been modified and twisted. What, then, had the heterosexual relationship of long ago really been like?—for there was no doubt it would return, once the mass production of eugenically acceptable males had been successfully accomplished, even though that might not happen in her lifetime. It was a fascinating poser, and it increasingly dominated her thoughts.

Crinila was a practical individual. As a freak, she had to be in order to make the most of a social order that rejected her, which was why, at an early age, she had determined to become highly proficient in the arts and techniques of love in a unisexual environment. But now she began to see the possibility of a new and daring practice—indeed, philosophy—which was not only timely but could conceivably form the basis of a new cult in keeping with the reversionist ethos—if reversion meant what it implied.

It was simple in essence but revolting in concept—though only insofar as it was alien to the conventions of the age. But, and this was the underlying strength of the idea, it was educational and evolutionary in a world which, in the foreseeable future, would need to adapt to the presence of men and the ways of men; and such education could hardly begin too soon.

First, however, it was necessary to use some of her trusted friends as a sounding board for her own particular brand of practical reversionism, and this she resolved to do discreetly, when suitable opportunities arose. True, they might be shocked, or feign to be shocked, but in fact the idea was as old as history itself and had been practiced in many cultures and societies, though never commonly or overtly, according to literature in the archives. In modern language it could be described as a simulation—a familiar word in a world in which simulation, in either practical or mathematical form, was an integral part of every new activity.

Meanwhile, a device, or perhaps "appendage" was the better word, had to be made in all its grotesque but functional detail—and here Crinila found herself rather at a loss. What detail? The ancient books in the archives were not as explicit as she would have liked; they presupposed some prior knowledge on the part of the reader. Nor were the illustrations particularly helpful, since the organ in question was always depicted in a flaccid non-mating condition. She managed to find some helpful diagrams, but even so, cross-sectional line drawings were hardly a working blue-print for a would-be sculptor. Some pictures of erotic carvings and statues from what was almost pre-history—ancient China, India, Egypt and elsewhere in the East—threw some light on the obscure scene, and, of course, one could extrapolate, as it were, from existing animals.

Eventually, after several months of research and some fascinating attempts at three-dimensional modeling in a light pliable plastic substance used in dental work, she decided that she had the geometry of the thing about right. But what about the size? That was a rather delicate matter, which necessitated some personal internal measurements and reference to contemporary books on gynecology and obstetrics. In the end, it was largely a matter of guesswork and common sense. The completed plastic prototype in what might be termed its "mating configuration" was a curious work of art indeed, and she wondered vaguely how any male could avoid feeling burdened and embarrassed by having such an unaesthetic object permanently attached to his anatomy. No wonder they used to keep it covered up so much.

The prototype itself was of no practical use, as the material was too soft and flexible. It was merely the rough model for a more refined sculpture in a firm but resilient plastic, which, she judged, ought to approximate to the reality—or rather, the reality which she as a female might comfortably accept. And that was about it. Fixing it in position presented little problem—a simple matter of elastic tapes and plastic cement.

Finally the thing was finished in all its repugnant glory. She stripped, put it on, and surveyed herself in a full-length mirror, frontally and in profile. Then she burst into hysterical laughter. It was just too ridiculous, and quite the funniest sight she had seen in years. The thing was an essay in incongruous deformity, and the soft swell of her pale breasts made the whole vision of unloveliness even more comic.

She sat down for a minute to compose her mind into a more serious and objective mood; then, covering her breasts with a cloth, just to be fair to her simulation of a man, she surveyed her image once more. This time she suppressed an urgent desire to laugh and scrutinized her reflection very closely, turning from side to side. One trouble was that the color of the plastic contrasted too redly against the translucent white of her albino skin, so that the appendage looked inflamed and angry —but in a subdued light that would not matter. Another was that the smooth, curving feminine shape of her body was quite incapable of creating an illusion of masculinity. She needed wider shoulders and narrower hips and a tough, angular ruggedness—plus (horrible thought) hair, on the arms, legs, chest, and even back. Given those things, the incongruity might not seem so hilarious.

However, it would do, and would almost certainly amuse friends, such as Girela and Marvin, once they had recovered their wits after the first visual impact of the transmogrified Crinila. Already she could hardly suppress her eagerness to have them visit her to explore the ludicrous possibilities of her new laughter-provoking toy. But not just yet. There was some preliminary pioneering work still to be done, so that she personally could gain experience in the proper and optimum use of the device and assess her own reactions and responses in subjective terms. The thought repelled her, but she was not a squeamish woman and could be stubbornly determined when she chose. And there was always the reassuring notion that what she was doing came under the heading of research. She, Crinila, the albino, was making her own personal contribution to the scientific infra-structure of reversionism and the acceptance once more of the male sex into an all-female humanity. She was not to know that she was to be the starting point of a new kind of perversion, which, accepted reluctantly at first, would spread rapidly by underground and clandestine routes throughout the world, to shake the stability of even Alpha-obsessed governments.

Chapter Twelve

Davana, the head of the Executive Committe of the Supervisory Council in Alphaville, died suddenly from a cerebral thrombosis when Alph was seventeen years old. Her body was removed to Lon for autopsy and cremation, and her place as chief executive was taken by a younger woman named Loron. She was of American origin and was known as a brilliant biogeneticist with particular qualifications in morbid psychiatry, which was the main reason for her new appointment. Koralin estimated that she was about the same age as herself, in her late thirties, and certainly younger and fresher than her colleagues on the committee, to whom she was now senior.

To Koralin a new face was as good as a new environment; it was as though a cool wind had risen to blow some of the staleness from the catacombs of Alphaville. Little had changed over the years. The boy had grown into adolescence and had reached the threshold of manhood without questioning his unceasing role as a donor of gametes, and with no apparent curiosity in anything other than the environment with which he had always been familiar.

Security had slackened. It was no longer necessary, now that male children existed in their thousands throughout the world. They, in a few years, would

reach the age when their seed would be used to conceive a second generation of males, at which point the
eugenic experts would be able to move in and exercise
their selective options. And so it would go on, generation after generation, and always more males and always better males, until . . .

Meanwhile, Alph was still the only existing source
of gametes, a fact of life which he seemed to accept
placidly without understanding. He was rugged and
handsome, and willing to be friendly with his clinically
objective mentors and guardians, but they kept their
professional distance from a creature which they still
regarded as an experiment. Their attitude was partly
a reflection of Davana's impersonal approach to Alph,
but now Davana had gone forever, and her successor,
if first impressions counted for anything, appeared to be
a warmer and more human kind of person.

There had been changes in the staff at Alphaville.
For some years, after it had been established that Alph's
progeny were healthy, normal and kicking infant boys,
the embargo on movement between the center and the
outside world had been lifted. Koralin, after an un-
fortunate period of hypertension and nervous break-
down, had been transferred to Lon for treatment and
convalescence. While there she had been honored by an
invitation to meet Galinia, the Head of State, in the
Silver Tower. Galinia had welcomed her with courtesy
and consideration, as if she were a visiting dignitary,
and there had been no sign of patronization.

Galinia had ushered her into a comfortable chair in
her private office. "Something to drink?"

"No, thank you, Mistress."

Galinia insisted. She took a bottle from a shelf and
poured some straw-colored liquid into a small glass.
"You look pale, child. This will put some color into
you. Drink it."

One could hardly refuse an order from the Head of

State, Koralin thought as she sipped the pungent fluid. It reminded her of anise, which she didn't much like.

Galinia sat down at her desk. "When your convalescence is over, which will be in four weeks, I understand, what do you plan to do, Koralin?"

"Return to Alphaville."

"Why? You have already been there for too many years, and there is no useful work for you to do on the project."

"Nevertheless, I feel involved. I wish to be associated with it—with the boy."

Galinia took a green-backed folder from the desk and referred to some papers within it. "As you seldom see the boy and have little access to him, the degree of involvement would seem to be minimal. Nor is your medical report reassuring. Your recent illness is attributed to neurosis resulting from a psychological conflict relating to the treatment of the boy. There was a dispute with Davana, for example . . ."

"Not a dispute—a discussion. I can see that Davana was right, but I feel that I, in my own way, was right, too. We were looking at a situation from different viewpoints—with different motivations."

"And you wish to return to Davana's regime."

"Yes, Mistress."

While Galinia glanced through further papers, Koralin sipped some more of the anise fluid. It was hot to her throat, but already she was beginning to feel more relaxed.

"I just know my place is there, for the present at least," she continued. "In my way, the boy is a part of my life."

"I can understand that," Galinia said, "though I am uneasy about the sentiment implied. I see from your dossier that you have no intimate friend among the women at Alphaville."

Koralin nodded.

"That is a frustrating and undesirable state. You are

a young and very attractive woman, and it is important
that you should form a sexual liaison with someone like
yourself."

"My status makes it difficult," Koralin explained. "I
am not of the staff and I am not of the executive;
therefore I do not really belong. I am, as it were, in
between ranks."

"Which surely is an admission that you have no
place in Alphaville. You are an anomaly."

Koralin shrugged. "It is not important."

"It is more important than you imagine," said Galinia. "I could, of course, veto your return, but that would
be an act of tyranny. I could have you accommodated
in conditions of luxury here in Lon, or wherever you
choose, with pleasant and interesting work to do—but
presumably that would not be your choice."

"That is so."

"Then I suggest a compromise. I will grant you a
three-month extension of your period of convalescent
vacation and introduce you to a hostess. You will live
with her, and she will see that you mix with entertain-
ing and amusing women. And if you should form a
deep liaison with somebody but still insist on returning
to Alphaville, then you may take your new friend with
you."

"You are generous, Mistress," Koralin said, "but I
should prefer to decline."

Galinia stood up and came closer to her. "On this
occasion I must be firm. I shall not permit you to decline. For a few months you will enjoy a normal
social life, without stress or isolation. It will be good for
you. And in the end you will be free to make your own
decision. Do you understand?"

"Yes, I understand—but . . ."

"No buts. Return to your apartment and I shall
arrange for your hostess to call on you in the early
evening. Regard her as a good friend, which is precisely what she will be."

Koralin thanked Galinia, but without great enthusiasm. As she was about to leave she was prompted to ask: "Why are you doing all this for me, Mistress?"

Galinia smiled. "Because without you, Koralin, there would never have been a reversionist government, and I would not be standing here now."

"I acted on impulse—not for reversionism." Koralin said.

"I know, and I sometimes feel that what the world needs is more action and less communication. That way we might get a great deal more accomplished. Well, make the most of your vacation while it lasts, and perhaps we may meet again in due course."

Koralin was hardly aware of the honor that had been conferred on her as she descended to street level in the high-speed elevator.

With the arrival of Loron to take charge, the atmosphere in Alphaville changed subtly. An air of relaxation became discernible in women who had formerly seemed tensely dedicated to their programmed tasks. A new informality softened the cold protocol of the rule-book. People actually began to *chat* instead of merely communicating, and jokes were actually made and laughed at. It was not that life had been intolerably stiff and formal under Davana's administration, but rather that it had been humorless and single-minded in its concentration on duty, and this had particularly affected Koralin, who in a sense had had no duty to concentrate on.

Alphaville was simply society as a whole in miniature, and Koralin thought it incredible that the behavior and indeed the spirit of people in the community should hinge so much upon the leader, and change with a change of leader. It was not that Loron had said or done anything to promote easier relationships; on the contrary, for the first week or so she was hardly seen at all as she plowed through masses of files and paperwork in her office in a crash effort to familiarize herself with the history of work at the center. She was just a relaxed person, recognizable as such in the same way that other people could be seen instantly to be irritable, highly strung, or neurotic.

One morning Loron called her first conference of the Central Executive Committee. Koralin, as usual, sat at the remote end of the table as a nonparticipating observer. Loron had no notes or papers in front of her —she spoke impromptu and conversationally.

"I expect you all realize," she said, "that Phase 2 of the Alpha Project has now, for all practical purposes, come to an end. The net result of Phase 2 at this moment is a world male population of just over fifteen thousand children and babies—all sons of Alph out there." She hooked a thumb towards the window on the assumption that Alph was somewhere in the sunlit gardens.

"There were a number of casualties. A few were stillborn, and others died from a virus infection similar to gastroenteritis, but in a much more virulent strain. We formed the conclusion that male infants tend to have a higher potential mortality rate than females— something we are looking into in our labs.

"The great majority of the first male generation are fit and healthy. They range in age from nearly eight years to just a few months, and some more births are scheduled just to button up the Phase 2 operation. For the moment we've got all we need to go ahead with Phase 3 in about a year or two from now.

"As you know, the big disadvantage of the first generation is that the genetic factor comes from one single source, i.e., Alph. That doesn't offer much scope for genetic selection. With Phase 3, however, the situation is different. We've got over fifteen thousand different genetic sources distributed all over the planet, which will give our eugenic geniuses something to get their teeth into.

"Phase 3 will follow much the same pattern as Phase 2. It will have its A and B aspects of the operation— that is, the filtering, inspection and despatch of male-forming gametes to Partho centers, and the selection of eugenically cleared young women for fertilization. There will, however, be an additional operation in which eugenic tests will be carried out on the DNA structure of the gamete chromosomes in order to get some kind of Keisintel standards and criteria established, or at least approximated to."

One woman remarked: "We have already had a preliminary briefing on Phase 3, Loron. What we'd like to know is where Alphaville fits into the plan."

"Alphaville is a dead duck," Loron said crisply. "By that I mean it won't be the Alphaville you've all learned to live with. The crisis is over. We've got fifteen thousand Alphs spread all over the place, and they don't need invisible fortresses for their protection. So Alphaville is being downgraded to the status of an ordinary Partho center allocated to Phase 3 of the project—just the same as all the other centers. With some modification to the structure and layout of the buildings, we'll be able to handle a female intake in batches of about fifty at a time—and, of course, we'll need to get rid of a lot of the existing staff because they'll be redundant."

"And what about Alph himself?" Koralin heard herself asking.

"Well, he's a dead duck, too. He's outlived his usefulness. We don't want his gametes any more—well, maybe just a few for preservation in the deep-freeze sperm banks. His eugenic standard is pretty low, and we wouldn't want to propagate any more from what he's got on his production line. We reckon we'll get better chromosomes from the first generation progeny."

"But what will happen to him?" Koralin insisted, her voice little more than a whisper.

Loron gave her a curious look. "That's a good question, Koralin. Candidly, we don't know yet. The computers came up with a blank, which means that so far as they're concerned Alph can be written off, so far as the project goes. They're too busy working on the other fifteen thousand Alphs to be bothered with the original. On the other hand, he *is* the original and he *is* unique. Half of the single cell from which he grew came from the world's last man to die more than five hundred years ago—an old man named Gavor. So Alph in his own right is a historic relic, which has to be preserved for posterity."

She paused and scratched her nose reflectively with an elegant finger. "I can tell you—practically every important museum and medical college in the world wants Alph, or a bit of him, either to inspect and analyze or encapsulate and exhibit in a glass case. He's in great demand, though he doesn't realize it."

Koralin suddenly felt quite dizzy and faint. She felt sure that she would fall from her chair. Her fingers were gripping the edge of the table so tightly that the knuckle bones showed white through the skin. Remotely she heard a voice asking a question, and she was glad that the attention of the others had been diverted from her while she regained her poise.

"What exactly does that imply, Loron? Euthanasia?"

"You mean murder," Loron said sardonically. "Let's use the right words; then there won't be any misunderstanding. No, I don't think Alph would like that very much."

"Why not a sex change," somebody suggested. "Then perhaps he could be integrated into society."

"Tricky. He's a very positive male. Anyway, he wouldn't like that either. Nor would the governments, museums and medical colleges. They want the first man preserved in his masculine state, not the first man converted into a woman. They wouldn't go for that at all."

"So what other options are open?"

"Precisely the same options as will be open for the fifteen thousand first-generation males when they, too, have outlived their usefulness as donors. And the second and the third generations, and perhaps more—totaling hundreds of thousands of males, maybe in the end even millions. The problem is not just Alph, but all his unsuitable and unwanted children and grandchildren. Until the first eugenically acceptable males begin to come off the assembly lines, all Alphs are expendable. In fact, they are an embarrassment in any civilized society such as ours."

"Have they been accorded human status in law?"

"Officially, no. That will have to await eugenic clearance."

"So the options remain open."

"For the time being, yes." Loron considered for a moment, her eyes somewhat speculative. "It is not unlikely that a special colony will be set up for redundant males when they have ended their term of duty as donors. It would be remote from inhabited areas and under tight security and guard—to keep them in, not to keep the rest of us out. That, too, has its disadvantages. We don't think it's a good idea to hold a large number of substandard and unwanted males in a kind of prison camp. We don't want to kill them off—not yet, anyway. We don't want to try converting them into females. Hell—that would be antireversionist, anyway! We're trying to make more men, not more women, and fake women at that. So what do we do? You tell me."

"Sterilization," somebody murmured.

"Plus freedom? What would be the point of that either biologically or eugenically in what will be for generations to come a fundamentally Lesbian society? It would be difficult to maintain proper control over the behavior of such men, even if sterile, if let loose in society. And it would tend to encourage certain decadent and depraved practices, known in vulgar terms as 'simulo,' which are causing concern to governments throughout the world: And all that totally ignores the economic aspect. What kind of useful work could substandard men, who have been deprived of intensive education in order to serve as donors, be expected to do in a complex matriarchal society such as ours? It will take a long time to find satisfactory answers to such questions. In the meantime, the problem is with us now."

A gloomy silence fell upon the committee. Koralin, who had now recovered from her transient spell of faintness, found herself repeating the word "simulo" in her mind. That stirred memories that took her back to Lon and the wild fantasy of her extended convalescence a few years earlier. And yet "simulo," decadent and depraved though it might be from the point of view of authority, was something fundamental seeking expression in darkened rooms behind locked doors, and in seedy clubs in dingy city streets. It was something that had a direct bearing on the problem of Alph and his countless offspring, whether the government liked it or not, and that could present a direct challenge to the dispassionate scientific planning of even a stable reversionist administration.

But that was not the immediate point. One could define and study the options indefinitely without arriving at a solution to the problem because one simple and arbitrary factor had been overlooked. It was the blind spot of contemporary society—the rod which the administration had made for their own backs. Although she was not officially a member of the committee, Koralin decided to state her views.

She stood up. That in itself was an error of procedure—while the chairman remained seated, so did everybody else—but she was determined to draw attention to herself so that what she had to say might carry more weight.

She said: "There is no problem in real terms. There is only an artificial problem in eugenic terms. The Alph and his Alphs are said to be substandard. Why? Because Keisintel's eugenic theory is assumed to be infallible. It is accepted as an axiom—the bible and statute book of our civilization. But by what absolute authority can Keisintel or any woman decree that certain genetic strains are desirable and others not?"

She hesitated for a moment, trying to collect her thoughts, aware that the others were staring at her aghast—with the sole exception of Loron, who merely eyed her intently, with a hint of a smile at the corners of her shapely lips. Then she continued:

"The Reversionist revolution happened for the very same reason, because the government of the day and its computers made an arbitrary decree. Destroy the male child, they said. We know what happened, but have we learned a lesson? Today the decree is to discriminate. Keisintel must be right, and therefore all human beings who fail to attain the eugenic standard she has prescribed are substandard rejects. That is eugenic discrimination—a crime far worse than the racial and religious discriminations of past history, for it embraces all people of whatever color or creed. Today the Keisintel rules decide who are our first-class and second-class citizens. But why should they? Without such rules there would be no rejected citizens and no embarrassing unwanted males."

She remained standing for a few seconds, not quite sure whether she had finished speaking or not, then nervously sat down. Immediately uproar broke out. The members of the committee voiced their shocked and angry reactions simultaneously in staccato words and phrases. Did she hear somebody shout "treason" and "subversion"? Only Loron had nothing to say during the hullabaloo, but when the noise began to subside she rapped sharply on the table with her knuckles.

"Order!" she commanded. The protests ceased, and all eyes turned to her.

"Thank you, Koralin," she said calmly. "You have stated with admirable clarity an additional option which most of us would have tacitly overlooked." She looked slowly at each member of the perturbed committee. "The additional option is to modify or even abandon the Keisintel eugenic regulations so that all human beings are equal and none can be discriminated against on genetic grounds. In such an event, there could be no justification for segregating the Alphs of this world from the female environment in which they were born, and there would be complete freedom of breeding. Okay? As an argument it sounds good. Of course, we'd still need to arrange for more male births than female in order to balance out the sexes. That can be done biochemically after fertilization."

A brief pause, then: "But there's one major snag with Koralin's option. It's illegal. It is contrary to both national and international law on eugenics, which is aimed at improving the physical and mental quality and performance of Homo sapiens by selective breeding. That law has been accepted throughout the world as a good and desirable law, and it is being enforced and implemented. It will, I predict, remain the law throughout the foreseeable future. So Koralin's option is not really an option at all."

Instant relief was visible on the faces of the committee, but Koralin sat silent and subdued. Loron continued: "In any case, as Koralin is not a member of the Central Executive Committee she has no brief to address the committee in any official capacity. In a formal and procedural sense, therefore, Koralin's option was not stated. I order it to be deleted from the record, and the single word 'interruption' substituted instead."

Then, looking directly at Koralin, she added: "Nevertheless, Koralin, I think that you and I ought to have an informal talk—perhaps immediately after this meeting. Meanwhile, I propose we continue with the agenda and leave the problem of the ultimate fate of Alph and his little Alphs to those best qualified to solve it."

The committee, having recovered from its traumatic shock, resumed its methodical deliberations.

Chapter Thirteen

"I can see," said Loron amiably, "that diplomacy is not your strong point, is it, Koralin?" She was sitting on the corner of the desk in her private room—a thing which Davana would never have dreamed of doing—while Koralin reclined in an easy chair near the window. Strange how one could feel instantly at ease with Loron, whereas in Davana's presence one had felt impelled to be cautious and circumspect.

Koralin smiled a little. "I have a sense of justice—of right and wrong."

"So does the judiciary appointed by the government, but I suspect that it would hardly go along with your views on Keisintel and eugenic discrimination. After all, the law is the law."

"There are good laws and bad laws."

"Well, that's as may be. Ordinary mortals like us can't change the law, so we have to learn to live with it and love it. And, if we're wise, we might try keeping certain controversial ideas to ourselves. Even a reversionist government can be sensitive about its permanence. There are currents moving beneath the surface of the water that are causing anxiety in the hierarchies of our world."

"You mean—like 'simulo'?"

"That and a few other things that seem to indicate

that our well-balanced Lesbian society, which took so long to create and stabilize is way ahead of government planning when it comes to adapting itself to the rebirth of the male sex. It's of interest that simulo emerged around the time of the first artificial inseminations in the Alpha 2B phase. In just a few years it has spread throughout the world, mostly under cover, but in some countries quite openly."

Koralin thought about that for a while. "It is not illegal," she pointed out.

Loron uttered a terse laugh. "It can hardly be illegal when it merely simulates what the administration is planning to introduce in the flesh, but not for a long time. The point is that it is undermining the whole Lesbian syndrome—in fact, the entire parthenogenetic syndrome itself. And, of course, it's a perversion."

"So is Lesbianism."

"That's debatable under the circumstances."

"It seems to me everything's debatable today," Koralin said. "We are born, and we grow up to accept laws and standards that we think are immutable and eternal and—this is the worst part—correct, in the godlike sense of infallibility. But it isn't so. There are no gods, and standards are set to resist change and establish uniformity. But things change just the same, and sometimes the biggest changes are brought about by small ideas—no more than that. Ever since the male child, Alph, was created, the pressure for change has been building up. It's not political. It has to do with life, death and birth—the whole business of being human and being normal. The government thinks it can legislate human instinct and emotion into submission—but it can't. It never will."

She leaned forward intently in her chair. "Do you know what simulo is, Loron? It is the stirring of the wombs of women throughout the world as their instincts begin to respond to the coming of men."

Loron nodded her head in a curious sideways fashion,

as though acknowledging and at the same time disputing the point. "You're quite a philosopher, aren't you, Koralin? Dangerous talk, too, particularly for a woman who was responsible for one revolution. Koralin is at it again, they will say."

"I'm sorry, Mistress," Koralin said. "There are things that seem so clear to me, and I try to explain them. . . ."

"You've already called me Loron and you don't have to call me Mistress. Right now we're equals. I think you're overrating simulo, at least in its conscious sense. It's a fad—and an irreverent fad, because it's mocking the government's earnestness about the Alpha Project. The government can't intervene without in effect saying 'You mustn't have artifical men—you've got to have real men, only by the time they've been eugenically cleared you'll all be dead, anyway. So stop it, you naughty girls.'"

"That's not really . . ." Koralin began, but Loron interrupted her and continued:

"There's an element of defiant irresponsibility about simulo—that's the unsettling thing that is worrying the administration. You see, the women of our world today are all, without exception, mono sexual by training and indoctrination. They would shrink in horror at the touch of a real living man, but to play with an artifact, a gruesome toy—well, it's amusing."

"It's more than that," Koralin said quietly. "I, too, was horrified at first, even with the toy, as you call it. I was angry, and filled with a sense of outrage and shame. And then, after the first reaction of the brainwashed mind had settled down, something strange happened. It is difficult to explain—quite indescribable. But . . . I went back, voluntarily, to be outraged again."

Loron stood up, stroking her lips with an extended forefinger, her manner intent and immensely serious. She came closer to Koralin. "You've had personal experience of this . . . thing?"

Koralin nodded. "Some years ago, when I was in Lon."

"Well, that's more than I can claim, and I'm supposed to be the psychiatric expert around here," said Loron, raising her eyebrows fractionally. She drew up a chair and sat facing Koralin. "Tell me about it, please. There's just you, me and the walls."

"I had been ill. I was sent to Lon for treatment and convalescence. I met the Head of State, Galinia, and she extended my vacation in the care of a hostess. I think she wanted me to form an emotional attachment, you know. Here at Alphaville I was alone and too obsessed with the boy."

"I know. I've read your dossier."

"Well, I found myself involved in an unending whirl of gaiety, amusements, clubs, parties and, if you like, orgies. Sometimes I lost track of my hostess, or she lost track of me, but always I was with beautiful and friendly women, somehow passing from one to another, like a passenger switching roundabouts. Looking back, it all seems like a crazy dream. If I was irresponsible —well, I was obeying the instructions of the Head of State, after all."

"And then?"

"One night in a club I met a girl named Girela. I remember her as a vivacious laughing girl. She asked me if I wanted to try a new experience—something fantastic. I was willing to try anything at that time. She said she had to call another friend, but later she took me back to her apartment, and we drank and caressed for a while, and undressed. And then . . ."

"Go on."

"Somebody came into the room. The light was very low and it was difficult to see clearly, but there was something odd—something quite impossible. It looked like a man, and yet . . . Next thing, Girela was holding me down on the divan, pinning my arms beneath while this male figure seized my legs and—raped me. Brutally, you know. Viciously. It went on and on and on and it hurt. I gave up struggling and surrendered, but still it went on. And then—there was this curious sensation, deep down here—she placed a hand on her pelvis—"not a hurt but just a hint of something else, something quite different. But suddenly it stopped. They released me, and Girela turned up the light."

"They laughed, of course."

"Yes. It was a great joke. The 'man' was a pretty young woman. She had a kind of tight plastic band around her chest to flatten her breasts, and she was wearing a very realistic plastic penis fastened around her buttocks. I had been terrified, but now I just felt ashamed and horrified.

"I can remember Girela saying . . . 'That's what reversionism is all about. It's a new game the government wants us to play. We've got to get some practice in before they send the real men around to do their stuff.' And something like—'It's great. You've got to learn to relax and close your eyes and make believe.' Then they did a demonstration in front of me. It was a combination of Lesbian techniques leading up to the fierce heterosexual part. I must say Girela seemd to be in a state of ecstasy, but all I felt at that time was disgust. I wanted to get away from the place. I went back to my hostess."

"Naturally there was a traumatic reaction," Loron commented, "but when you'd had time to think about it . . ."

"Oh, the reaction lasted quite a long time—more than a week. I tried to forget the experience. I deliberately sought the normal Lesbian relationship, but somehow it didn't seem the same any more. I don't know why. It just didn't seem real. So I went back to Girela and her friend, whose name was Marvin, and through them I met another skilled exponent of the simulo art. She was a beautiful albino woman named Crinila. It was with her that I first experienced a true vaginal orgasm. It was indescribable—something I had never had before."

Koralin hesitated, her eyes withdrawn and dreamy "There's nothing more to tell. Some weeks later I left Lori and the dreamworld and returned here. The simulo thing was in its early days then. I believe it was Crinila who started it. But I can understand how and why it has spread so rapidly. It really is a new sensation."

"Not so new," Loron remarked. "It's as old as history. Only the context is new. That and the fact that the practice is interwoven with some rather sensitive political considerations. Anyway, thank you, Koralin. I'm grateful for your very candid account—not that it will do anything to help the Alphs of this world."

"Is there *anything* that can be done while the Keisintel rules still apply?" Koralin asked. "You say they are not educated, and that is true, but it is our fault. Alph's education was deliberately restricted to a very elementary grade, because his only recognized function was that of a gamete machine. Now he is to be discarded as useless, but he could still be educated to a much higher level—to understand the nature of the world into which he was brought without his knowledge. You cannot condemn ignorance."

"I do not condemn anything, Koralin, least of all Alph."

"Then what will happen to him?"

"I thought we had been through all that during the meeting. He will be phased out, quite quickly. What to do with him is another matter, and the options have to be decided at a much higher level. Meanwhile, he will stay here—a rather bored and idle Alph, I fear, until instructions are received from the hierarchy. I fancy it will be the prison camp concept that will win in the end, but not for Alph all alone. That allows a leeway of many years, perhaps a decade, until Phase 3 is exhausted and Phase 4 begins. Plenty of time for thinking and planning, analyzing social trends and introducing new legislation."

"Couldn't we make some attempt to provide further education for Alph—just to test his capacity and see what can be done? He seems intelligent enough."

Loron shook her head. "It's not allowed for in the project."

"I mean, unofficially. Some regular tuition to keep him occupied."

"If he chooses to be kept occupied. Idle habits are hard to break down. You could hardly force him to cooperate."

"I think he would *want* to cooperate," Koralin insisted. "At the moment he's just a vegetable."

"Stud animal, you mean. Anyway, it's impractical. There's no incentive and no motivation, and we have no authorized or qualified teaching staff. We're all too busy."

"I'm not busy," Koralin said. "I'm just an observer, here by privilege. For the first time I could do something productive and useful."

Loron eyed her sceptically. "Can you teach?"

"I can try."

"What would you teach?"

"All I know. Slowly—step by step. If it worked, then perhaps professional teachers would be allowed to take over. If it failed—there's no loss and no harm done."

"Mm—I wouldn't be so sure," Loron murmured doubtfully. "I can anticipate serious difficulties already. I think the answer's got to be a very firm no. Our job is to implement Project Alpha—no more, no less. Further education doesn't come into it at this stage. Sorry, Koralin—though it's not a bad idea."

Koralin's disappointment was only too apparent in her forlorn expression, but there was nothing she could say.

"On the other hand," Loron continued, "since Alph

is going to have a great deal of spare time on his hands, there would be no objection to talking to him. One could broaden his horizons and extend his limited knowledge without actually doing what could be defined as teaching. One could leave him to take the initiative by asking questions—but exactly how they were answered might call for tact and caution. Don't forget that Alph has no knowledge of the outside world. He knows nothing of history or science or even Project Alpha. Or sex itself, for that matter. It might be better to leave him in ignorance. The wrong answers could do a lot of damage."

"But you said there would be no objections to talking to him."

Loron smiled. "He has been talked to and at ever since he was capable of understanding speech—by you yourself as well as other members of the staff. There is no official embargo on *that*—but there are constraints of the kind I have outlined."

"I understand."

"Well then—talk to him if you wish, but I cannot authorize a formal program of teaching as such. And don't forget that other matters take priority. There is a rigid schedule for sleep, meals, medicals and psycho tests—not to mention the possibility of some further gamete sampling if called for."

Koralin nodded. Behind the other woman's non-committal words she could sense a tacit approval, but not necessarily an unmotivated approval. What Loron seemed to be hinting was that she would be interested to see how Alph responded to further education, but that it could not officially be recognized as such, and could only be conducted within the rules of the game by a subterfuge. To Koralin that was a green light. Loron might only wash her hands of the matter, and could truthfully say that she had vetoed it, but the psychiatrist within her was unwilling to allow a unique experiment of this type to go by untried. Yes, Koralin understood only too well—or at least she thought she understood.

During the next few days Koralin made no attempt to approach the boy—she still thought of him as a boy although he was now a young man, tall and lithe of build, lazy because he was never required to be anything other than lazy, and a little stubborn and arrogant in manner, which was not unusual in adolescents of whatever sex. But she watched him from the window of her room when he was in the gardens or the woodland beyond, and she watched him through the polarized glass panels that allowed unseen observation during medicals and exercise sessions in the indoor gymnasium and the underground swimming pool. His naked body fascinated her, but it was a cold unthinking fascination, for she suppressed all reaction or response before it could form within her. Bored instructors were always present during exercise, but they did not participate; they had long since stopped training him. He was athletic enough but never seemed to exert himself more than he had to. After all, why should he?

Meanwhile she was turning over and over in her mind an approach to education that would fall within the terms of reference laid down by Loron, so that she could truthfully say it was no more than a conversation, without admitting that the conversation was one-sided and carefully planned to impart information. It would not be difficult—though precisely what information she had in mind was by no means clear to her.

She checked Alph's regular schedule of activity. Medicals generally took place in the mornings and exercise in the afternoons, though this was not always

so and could be varied by bad weather, gamete operations and so on. Usually the late afternoons and evenings were blank. She calculated that on the average
she could have free access to Alph for about four hours
a day if she wished, although in practice she would
not need so much time.

When to start—that was the only remaining point of
decision. For some strange reason she found herself
curiously reluctant to make up her mind. It was as if
there were some enormous mental inertia to overcome,
and she even found herself wondering, when it came
to the point, whether she really wanted to undertake
the further education of Alph at all. It was an inhibition
that defied analysis, and because of that it troubled her.

Loron said no, she argued, however much she may
have provided unofficial loopholes afterwards. She said
she foresaw difficulties. But I have talked with Alph
many times before, and there were no difficulties. If she
had said yes I would not hesitate, but as it is, the responsibility is on my shoulders.

She studied her face in a mirror. Still pretty, but
pale. Traces of anxiety in the curve of her lips, and a
certain gauntness under those high cheek bones. Her
hair needed more lacquer. But the overall effect was
intelligent and feminine—and, she thought, pleasing.
But pleasing to whom? Herself, other women, or Alph?
It was a disquieting question.

And yet deep down in her mind she knew exactly
what it was she wanted of Alph, but the primitive urge
was never permitted to rise to the restless surface of her
consciousness.

Chapter Fourteen

Lycia was requisitioned three times by the State for duty under the Project Alpha program. Between each birth she was allowed to return to university for a year to resume her studies, but nevertheless her academic life was severely disrupted. Additionally, she was severed from old friends and colleagues and was forced into establishing new relationships—and here she ran headlong into unexpected barriers.

In simple terms, she discovered that she was being disparagingly referred to as "Superwoman," or a "Keisintel Special." These same sneers were being equally applied to the other young women who had passed the stringent eugenic tests required to participate in the male birth program. Throughout the country relatively few women—less than two hundred—had qualified, and the proportion was roughly the same in other countries. From Lycia's point of view, while it was gratifying to know that she was one of the eugenically perfect minority, it came as a disconcerting shock to learn that this accolade created resentment and hostility among other women—the rejected majority.

In Lycia's case the gulf was aggravated by the fact that she was selected three times, whereas the usual duty requirement was twice, and this obviously indicated a very superior eugenic standard indeed. Only in the

Partho center, among other chosen women, was life tolerable and normal. Outside she had no friends any longer. Even Crinila's attitude had changed. Her thinking was different, and in an odd way even dangerous. For perhaps the first time in her life Lycia was conscious of a real and frightening sense of insecurity.

Crinila was cordial enough but made it quite plain to Lycia that she was not prepared to resume the romantic relationship that had ended with the idyllic holiday in Europe so many years ago. "You and I are different people now, Lycia," she explained, still her pale, translucent, beautiful self, but discernibly older, and tired around the eyes. "The world itself is different. In the last six years you have spent half the time in sheltered comfort, cut off from real events."

"I can understand that," said Lycia, "but why am I treated like an outcast? I have done nothing that the State did not order me to do."

"It is *we* who are the outcasts, not you and your other Superwomen," Crinila said with acerbity. "But listen to me talking! I was always an outcast from birth —an albino, a genetic freak. I often wonder why they allowed me to live. Now I have company, because there are millions of outcasts. The Keisintel rejects. Substandard citizens."

Lycia's voice began to show signs of strain and impatience. "That is nonsense. Keisintel has been the law for nearly two hundred years, and eugenic selection has been going on for many generations—but there has never been any hint of *class* feeling about standard or substandard citizens."

There was cynicism in Crinila's half smile. "Because nobody knew which was which—apart from the obvious throw-outs like me, who happily have a rarity value. It was all anonymous. We all did our two tours of duty in the Partho centers, produced our anonymous daughters, and never saw them again. They went to the State nurseries to be graded and filtered for further selection breeding when they matured. They say the infant mortality rate for hopeless rejects is very high. And as for the rest of us who survive—well, some are more eugenic than others. And now, for the first time, we know who the Superwomen are—and they are the privileged ones who will produce the Supermen. The same process of selection will be carried out on the Alpha males, but what will happen to the rejects? Is our splendid Superworld of the future to be inhabited only by the Superchildren of Superwomen and Supermen?"

"Whyever not?" Lycia asked in genuine perplexity. "If one accepts Keisintel's principles for refining the human species . . ."

"If one accepts Keisintel's principles!" Crinila sneered. "What right did Keisintel have to refine anything? By what law of nature is one human inferior to another because she doesn't quite match up to Keisintel's equations? It is unjustifiable and degrading discrimination between people with an equal right to survive and reproduce their kind."

Her flash of anger subsided abruptly. "I'm sorry, Lycia. You've been out of touch, and now nobody will communicate with you because you are one of *them*."

"Them?"

"The Superpeople who think they're going to inherit the earth."

"I'm *not* a Superperson," Lycia said. She sounded tired and dispirited. "Nor do I know if any of the three sons I bore will be Superpeople. I will never know who they are or where they are. Frankly, I don't care. It all sounds to me very childish and subversive, but I can't change the law any more than you can."

"Don't be too sure," said Crinila quietly. "Perhaps I and ten million others can. Nature is a weird old bird. We have already seen a powerful totalitarian government overthrown by reversionists, but nature can arrange its own reversions better than any planned computerized administration, and without apparent logic. We thought the revolution was over when the reversionists came to power, but that was only the start of it. The real revolution is biological, and that takes no account of governments or computers. The so-called parthenogenetic syndrome is crumbling, and the Lesbian mythology along with it. Sorry? It served its purpose. Keisintel, too. She's already dead, in more ways than one, but the Establishment hasn't got around to realizing it yet."

"That is seditious talk, Crinila. What's come over you? I remember the times when . . ."

"So do I, Lycia, my old love." The words were gentle, but there was irony in the inflection. "It's nice to live in the past, but there's an urgent present to be lived in, too, and a future to be built."

Perhaps Crinila was right, Lycia thought, but she seemed to be making a hysterical fuss about nothing in particular. As for the Keisintel laws—surely it was better to improve the human species than just let it run wild? She had no wish to be bothered with questioning the validity of such specious arguments. She only wished to live in peace and harmony with her fellow citizens, if only they would allow her to—but they wouldn't even do that. She was a Superwoman.

Lycia continued to visit Crinila on occasions, mainly because her friend was a kind of straw by which she could still cling to a receding humanity, although there was no longer any question of erotic liaison. It was during one of these visits that she met, quite by accident, Girela and Marvin and two other women. They had all been drinking, and she felt as if she had gatecrashed an uninhibited party. Although she had made it clear that she would be happy to leave, having arrived without warning, they all insisted that she should stay and join in the merriment.

Lycia suspected that there was more to the merriment than met the eye. She was not fond of alcoholic drink, but took some to be sociable. It was clear, like water, with a pungent bitter taste. It probably contained hallucinatory drugs, she thought warily.

For a while she remained an observer, listening to meaningless gay chatter and, here and there, some serious talk with political undertones. Although she drank very slowly, Girela, who seemed the merriest and most vivacious of them all, kept filling up her glass, and presently her head seemed to be detached from her body and floating in space. Colors sparkled with luminous intensity, as if they had been siphoned from a rainbow. It was an extraordinary pleasant sensation —all she wanted to do was drift towards the colors like a small white cumulus cloud.

A hand took hers and squeezed it gently. It was Crinila—an incredibly lovely, pure white Crinila, with pale pink eyes that seemed to glow with warmth. She could not restrain the emotional electricity that trembled like static within her—but it was still not the Crinila she recalled from long ago, and behind her the other women were laughing and talking quietly with the air of conspirators.

"It's time for party games," Crinila said. "We want you to join in. We've never played with a Superwoman before."

That sounded ominous and threatening in a veiled way, but Lycia's mind was fuddled, and she could not think straight. "No," she said, "I think I'd rather sit here for a while. I—I feel rather dizzy."

"Excellent!" Crinila laughed. "You'll enjoy it all the more. Come on."

Another woman took her other arm, and together they pulled her out of the chair. True, she *was* dizzy, but it was the pleasing sensation of being in a gently undulating boat turning in wind and current.

"We'll go into my bedroom," said Crinila. "Girela—you can be Superman."

They all laughed as if at some privately shared joke. The sense of inner caution prompted Lycia to draw back. Crinila was no longer an intimate friend, and the other women were strangers. But they were holding her firmly by the arms, and somebody else had taken her waist from the back and was pushing.

In a moment she was propelled against her will into Crinila's familiar bedroom. Almost immediately the light faded to a subdued glow in which furniture and people became colorless shapes and oddly blending contours.

"Across the bed," said Crinila. It was a general instruction to the others.

Lycia struggle to collect her thoughts and resolution, but she was lost and afraid, and her protests were drowned by excited chatter and laughter. In sudden alarm she realized that they were stripping off her clothes. Instinctively she thrust her body about in an attempt to break loose, but that only seemed to excite them all the more. Groping fingers clutched at her and dragged at her skirt—and then she was naked and pinned down, arms and legs firmly secured by the grip of determined fingers and the weight of eager bodies.

"Relax and enjoy yourself," Crinila whispered close to her ear. "This is going to be fun—even for a Superwoman."

Somebody new had come into the room, walking with slow measured steps towards the bed. It had to be Girela—but in the gloom it didn't look like Girela, or even a woman. The body was naked and flat, without breasts, but lower down she could see something gross and obscene. But no—it couldn't be . . .

She screamed as the assault began, then hands stopped her mouth and stifled her. There was nothing she could do but tense herself to endure the unrelenting violence that went on interminably until, weak and exhausted, she collapsed limply into total submission.

They released her and left her lying on the bed. She did not move and was incapable of thought. Gradually, through noise and laughter and a periodic vibration and shaking of the bed, she became aware that the game was continuing—the others were taking turns among themselves and changing partners. She knew what it was now, of course—simulo, a word she had heard mentioned with a snigger from time to time without understanding its true significance. Well, she had been ruthlessly and efficiently educated by experience and felt totally dejected and humiliated.

In due course the light brightened. The game had ended, and now the women were dressing, apparently tired and relaxed by their exertions. Crinila came over to her and helped her to sit up, patting her cheek gently as one might do to a sulking child.

"Cheer up, Lycia. Put your clothes on and come and have another drink. We'll start a new party."

Lycia said nothing, but dressed apathetically, in no great hurry. Her face was set in an expressionless mask —taut, but under control now, even though her mind remained blank and reactionless. She recognized the anesthetic effect of shock; for the present its deadening effect was welcome.

After a while she went into the other room, where the drinking had started again, but now there were two more guests—attractive brown-skinned girls of African origin. Obviously it was a party that was destined to continue into the long weary hours of early morning, and she wanted no part of it.

Crinila came over to her, smiling, friendly and overamiable, as though trying to conceal guilt and remorse. "Have a drink, Lycia," she offered. "It will make you feel better."

Lycia shook her head. "It's late. I must go."

"Just one drink. You need it, don't you? Be honest with yourself."

"Well, all right." Crinila was right—she did need it. She needed anything that would keep her mind dead. But in this instance the drink didn't really help; her depression increased in the atmosphere of rising gaiety.

"You mustn't take it so seriously," Crinila was saying above the random noise of voices. "It's always a bit of a shock the first time, but after a while it grows on you. Let's be honest—that's what Project Alpha is all about in the long run, so what's wrong with getting used to the idea now by simulations? There's nothing illegal about it, and if anything is a perversion it's the Lesbian syndrome they forced us into from childhood."

"I'm not arguing the point," Lycia said. "I'm just tired. I need to sleep."

"You can sleep here."

"No—I must get back to the university. I'm very late already."

She had her way in the end, and left without saying goodbye to anyone other than Crinila. The cool air of the street made her head swim after that final drink, so that she walked slowly and carefully, as if along a narrow plank. Three blocks further on she leaned against a wall and was sick. A dark cloud obscured her brain as fatigue drained her body of energy. She was not aware that she had already slumped to her knees.

"We found her unconscious on the pavement near Intersection 14," said the police patrolwoman. "She'd been sick. Better check her over—oh, and she's been drinking ambrosia by the smell, so you'd better test for drugs, too."

The young medico in the hospital casualty department turned up her nose in distaste for an instant. "Right."

"She's a student at the university. Name of Lycia. A eugenic Alpha three times according to her papers."

"Mm—well, she doesn't look very eugenic right now," the medico remarked. "I'll let you have a report as soon as I can."

She switched on the light above the trolley as the policewoman left the room.

An hour later the duty officer at the district police headquarters duly received the hospital report on video, with a paper printout for filing. She read it in the deadpan way that policewomen did and thumbed a switch on the desk intercom.

"Belex?"

"Yes."

"Can you come in?"

"Yes."

A non-uniformed policewoman entered the office. The duty officer handed her the printout. "Casualty in District General Hospital. Picked up unconscious in the street. That gives you the full check-out. It's a drug case—also bruising of limbs, sexual assault, some internal lesions. Could be a forced simulo. No previous record. She's a eugenic Alpha, which helps us. We've got to pin this one down and make it stick. She's got to talk as soon as she's conscious—drugs if necessary. The medico will fix it."

The policewoman sighed. "It doesn't improve, does it? I'll get around there right away and check back as soon as there's any hard information."

The duty officer nodded and switched off the video.

Lycia remembered very little of her brief stay in the hospital. They released her on the following day, but meanwhile there had been hours of talk and questions and answers with a woman sitting at her bedside, whose face she could hardly remember. She could recall virtually nothing of the dialogue—except for odd references to drinking and that horrid word "simulo," and Crinila's name had been mentioned. That worried her a little, for she had no wish to cause trouble for an old friend, no matter how her personality and character had changed.

The medico was uncommunicative. "You were brought in by the police," she said curtly. "Unconscious in the street. The police asked you a few questions. That's all."

"When you examined me . . ." Lycia suggested tentatively.

"Intoxication. Some bruises. You needed to sleep it off. You can go now. You're discharged."

That was as much information as she was likely to pump out of the medico, who seemed resentful of her presence in the hospital at all. She washed and dressed, checked out of the hospital, and returned to the university, going straight to her room and cutting lectures for the day. She lay down on her bed to think, not focusing her mind on anything in particular, but letting it run freewheel. Funny how a person could change so much in just a few years. Society itself, for that matter. There was a new substratum of different people around—decadent people determined to tear down conventions and established moralities, and the pity of it was that Crinila had become inextricably mixed up with them. Perhaps she was a weak character after all, though Lycia had always thought of her as strong—if only in her courageous ability to face the world as an albino and succeed. Only now she hadn't succeeded; and had been dragged down into a dangerous underworld, which must sooner or later produce a disciplinary backlash from authority.

And as for the simulo game—well, everyone to her

own taste in a tolerant society, but she suspected that society wasn't really all that tolerant. In any case, violence was violence, whatever you called it, and presumably rape by a simulated man was as criminal an act as rape by a real man—if one existed outside of the Alpha male. Perhaps simulo was the shape of things to come, but for another century or more it would remain a world without men, until the geneticists and eugenic scientists were ready to establish the new bisexual order of society. Until then there was nothing to be gained by undermining the stability and security of a civilization that had survived and flourished without men for hundreds of difficult years.

Crinila was wrong, and so were her friends; but to convince them of that called for more persuasive argument than she was capable of mustering. Also, as "Superwoman" and a "Keisintel Special" she was at a psychological disadvantage even before she could start arguing; if anything, they regarded her as part of the Establishment.

It was difficult and depressing, and there seemed to be no glimmer of light in the dark shrouded skies that lay ahead. After university, what? A job, somewhere, and her cachet would travel with her wherever she went. Here comes "Superwoman"—keep out of her way, put her on the black list. In the final analysis, only Crinila remained—a changed Crinila, but still by definition a friend, compared with hostile masses.

At that moment the videophone buzzer sounded and a red light winked above the screen. She got up and pressed the communication button, wondering who could possibly be calling her, unless it was Crinila herself. The face that appeared on the screen was vaguely familiar, but it wasn't Crinila—then she recognized it as one of the girls she had met briefly in Crinila apartment, and who had taken part in her violent initiation into the art of simulo. Her name, she thought, was Marvin.

"Lycia," said Marvin in a quiet voice filled with venom and loathing, "you are a vicious, treacherous toad. You deserve to be tortured and torn apart." The thin mouth, drawn tight with hate, spat at the screen. "If I get half a chance I'll tear you apart myself."

"For God's sake," Lycia cried in panic, "what have I done? What's happened."

"*You* know what's happened, you evil cow. They've arrested Crinila and Girela and the others on drug and violence charges, and they'll make it stick because you blabbed to the police. They've got 'Superwoman' as chief witness, so they can't fail now, though they've been gunning for Crinila for years and failed every time. Aren't you proud of yourself, you filthy rotten . . ."

Lycia switched off the video with trembling fingers, quite taken aback but suddenly calm—strangely calm. Of course; it made sense. The police had interrogated her in the hospital. They had used truth drugs, no doubt. They'd probably been after Crinila for some time over the simulo business, but though it was frowned upon it wasn't illegal. Violent assault was, and she suspected that there had been hallucinogenic drugs in those drinks she had taken. Yes—they'd got Crinila. The others didn't matter. They'd got Crinila, the seditious opponent of the Keisintel laws, and they'd see she got the full treatment. Psychological reorientation, they called it. That simply meant that nobody would ever see her again.

And all because of me, she thought. If I hadn't gone around there, if I hadn't forced myself back into her life when she made it plain that she didn't want me, this would never have happened. Marvin is right. I'm a vicious, treacherous Keisintel Special. I betrayed my oldest friend. Chief witness? No.

She went into the bathroom and committed suicide in a very old-fashioned and relatively painless way. She locked the door and filled the bath, adding a little tinted perfume. Then she lay for a while in the warm soothing water, not bothering to think any more. All thinking was done. When she was comfortable and drowsy she slashed her wrists to the bone with a sharp knife. The water became crimson as her life drained away.

Chapter Fifteen

The education of Alph began in a tentative, nervous way. Koralin, despite many days of thinking, planning and self-analysis, did not really know how or where to start. Her aim initially was to be conversational in a generalized sense, to get some kind of dialogue in motion, and then gradually and systematically lead it round to a subject about which Alph knew little or nothing, and so, over a period of time, fill in the gaps in his knowledge. There would be no compulsion on Alph to participate at all—indeed, she had no authority or power to command cooperation—but his own natural curiosity and a growing awareness of his ignorance must surely compel his attention.

It was an approach that could hardly come into conflict with the broad negative policy hinted at by Loron. There was no program and no curriculum—just an ad hoc stick-and-carrot approach which, being informal, would not be documented or recorded. But in practice it didn't work out at all well. For one thing, Alph was not a great conversationalist; and for another, she got the impression that he was already too old and too inflexible in his naive ideas to extend his horizons—particularly if it involved mental effort. There was always the inherent trait of laziness to be overcome.

Alph, at the age of seventeen, was already bearded,

though the beard was no more than a soft downy fur that covered his chin and upper lip and the sides of his face. It was light brown in color—not nearly so dark as the lank brown hair on his head—so that at a distance it was hardly visible, except as a discoloration. There had been a serious debate at executive committee level about Alph's beard: Let it grow naturally or shave it off? Since agreement could not be reached it had been decided to wait until the beard was longer and stronger and then review the situation. After all, a beard was a secondary sexual characteristic and an important symbol of differentiation.

He was tall—around six feet—and reasonably well built, slender rather than husky. He possessed all the awkward grace of an adolescent, with a hint of the hard poise that was yet to develop fully. Koralin couldn't have said whether she thought him handsome or not, never having seen a living man before, but she found the shape of his face, rather long and bony, quite pleasing. His eyes were of an indeterminate color, predominantly grey but flecked with green when you looked closely. His general mien was relaxed and thoughtful, almost contemplative in the philosophical sense, though he could spring into tense activity on an impulse. The brittle energy was there, stored quietly inside him, awaiting the instant of discharge like a high-voltage spark between powerful electrodes.

Which was why, she thought, one tended to feel irrationally uneasy in his company, even when he lazed in his most idle moments and ignored what was being said to him. Alph the child and Alph the young man were really two different creatures, a point that could be easily overlooked by someone who had had to grow up with him, day after day and year after year.

Still, he was good-natured and never complained. What had he to complain about anyway? All that had ever happened to him was his normal way of life, and there was nothing he could compare it with, except the unceasing industry of his attendants with their strange instruments and machines. Did he ever wonder what they were up to? He probably didn't care.

A typical conversational gambit: "Hello, Alph. It's hot today. Have you been swimming?"

"Yes."

This would be in the garden under the blazing mid-afternoon sun, with Alph still wearing his skirt, although the cape had been discarded.

"What did you eat for lunch?"

"Some mixture—like rice and fish."

"Good?"

A quick smile. "Well, I ate it."

There was a certain sublety in that simple statement when you thought about it—tact and wry humor.

"Did you ever think where fish come from?"

He shrugged. "Water. I've seen some in the stream over there. Little fish."

He meant the minnows in the narrow stream that trickled through the woodland beyond the garden. The stream was one of his favorite haunts; the burbling movement of the clear water seemed to exert a hypnotic fascination over him.

"Those are tiny fish—too small to eat. The big fish that we eat come from the great seas and oceans."

"I don't know about seas and oceans. They are part of the wild land beyond the wall."

"It is not so wild as you think. There are people beyond the wall."

Another grave shrug. "I know. They go to catch fish and animals and other things to make machines inside the wall. I see them when they fly over the wall." He pointed to the sky, where aircraft and helicopters occasionally followed the glide path to the small airstrip a mile or so distant.

"Yes, but there are people who live beyond the wall all the time. Very many people. Millions of people. They live in big towns much bigger than Alphaville."

A sidelong glance from sceptical grey eyes. "Oh, but that is not so. All people live inside the wall. Outside there is only wild land, and it is dangerous." A new thought and a half smile. "You are joking because you think I am a fool."

"No, you are not a fool, and I am not joking. Outside the wall is a big world of people and towns and countries and oceans. One day I will show you, if I can."

"I have seen already. They have taken me outside the wall. It is wild land. Green, with trees and hills, and there are animals and birds, but no people live there."

"Yes, that is true. Alphaville is surrounded by wild land. But further on, much farther on, there is blue water, for Alphaville is on an island. And beyond the blue water are many islands and many people."

"It is not so. I have seen the wild land, but there is no blue water. Anyway, water is white, like in the swimming pool and the stream. Even you have never seen blue water."

"I have sailed in a boat across blue water, and I have been to the other lands and lived with other peoples. They are real."

"Oh, yes. In your mind they are real, like a dream. I do not believe in your blue water. Show me some."

"I would have to take you to see it, and it is very far away."

"There. You see, I am not so simple."

It was always like that, a kind of mental war of attrition to break down the barricades of a closed mind. The scientists and psychologists had done their work well. Pictures, books and films would have helped enormously, but of course they had been deliberately struck off Alph's educational inventory. Perhaps it would be possible to get hold of some photographs or maps, or any material evidence—though that might contravene even Loron's flexible regulations.

As time went by Koralin realized that there was no easy way to discredit Alph's complacent acceptance of the total world within the wall. To him it was logical and made good sense, and he saw no reason to question the absolute authority of his earlier mentors. Apart from which, he shared with many brilliant scientists and philosophers, albeit unknowingly, a strong preference for a simple explanation rather than a complex one. His small world was rational enough, and he saw no need to accept stories that could not be substantiated about a vaster and more complicated world. "Show me some blue water," he had said, just as an atheist might say "Show me God." Why complicate simplicity?

There was one sure way in which she knew she could shatter his psychological defense mechanism, but it was hazardous and she was afraid, for she found herself unable to predict the result. It could wait. There were still many avenues to explore before venturing to tackle the most fundamental deceit of all, when she could offer visible and tangible evidence that she was right—that what she said was so, and that he was wrong. First she had to work out all the implications and ramifications of what she would ultimately have to do, and unless she could remain in control of the situation—and in control of herself as much as Alph—then her career, her liberty, and perhaps even her life might be in jeopardy. And that applied equally to Alph, in all his childish innocence.

So she persisted in the daily conversations about generalities, which got precisely nowhere. History failed. Alph could not really visualize a past any more than a future, except in abstract terms, which was, in a sense, curiously sophisticated. For him, time was something you measured with a clock, just as you measured space with a ruler. To say he was seventeen years of age was no more significant than telling him he was six feet tall.

That humans were created from a seed was self-evident. So were plants and animals, but he had no knowledge of sex or its function in fertilization. Seeds were drawn from the body in tubes and used to create tiny babies which grew and grew. It was done to everybody, they had told him, and to animals, too. It seemed simple and logical, and he saw no reason for disbelief.

That was the point at which Koralin could have turned the subject to her own advantage and delivered the *coup de grace* to Alph's kindergarten beliefs in his childlike world of uncomplicated fantasy; but she let the opportunity go by default. It was too soon. Perhaps it would always be too soon. She felt that she did not yet have enough self-assurance and relaxed poise to carry it off with a proper sense of detachment, while at the same time she recognized that what was really required was not detachment but involvement. While that conflict remained in her mind she was not ready for the desired but dreaded practical experiment.

And so the days passed aimlessly by. Alph was probably learning a great deal in a negative fashion, in the form of an unacceptable background mythology concerning oceans and blue water, about cities and sciences and millions of people, about aircraft and ships and machines, and the sun and the stars. He rejected them as one might reject the intangibles of ghosts and goblins and witchcraft, but the information would remain on file for future reference. In that sense Koralin felt that her efforts were not in vain; sooner or later fragments of the diverse data would add up and perhaps assume significance and reality to Alph.

One thing that was undeniably happening—and oddly enough she was unaware of it at first—was her own rapidly increasing importance in Alph's total life. Although she made a habit of visiting him in the late afternoons and early evenings as regularly as possible, she was not immediately conscious of the change that had taken place in his daily program. True, Loron had said that he had become, in effect, redundant, but she had also indicated that the daily schedules would continue as before. In fact, they were rapidly dropped. Things were happening in Alphaville that took a long time to reach Koralin's ears.

The first step was a progressive withdrawal of the majority of the staff and a redeployment of the remainder. At the same time architects, surveyors and engineers moved in to design a new expanded Alphaville to function as an updated Phase 3 center. Alph was no longer a focus of interest or attention, and Loron received specific instructions to abandon all aspects of the Alph operation and to hold him under existing conditions of security with minimal supervision pending further instructions regarding his disposal.

So the medicals and controlled exercise sessions were dropped. His special meals were replaced by portions from the main catering center. A woman was assigned to act as a casual part-time "housekeeper" to attend to routine matters of accommodation, cleaning, laundry, and so on, while a medico looked in about once a week to check that the forgotten man was still alive.

That Loron had not informed Koralin of these changes was simply because Koralin was far from her mind. As a supernumerary and non-official resident, Koralin had not been the subject of movements, postings, or instructions of any kind. Moreover, there were certain political undertones in the proposed rebuilding of Alphaville which were absorbing Loron's shrewd attention—she sensed that all was not well in the great outside world. It was not until Koralin requested an audience with her that she remembered the curious conversation about "further education" for Alph, and now it all seemed so irrelevant.

She granted Koralin a few brief minutes one morning and immediately apologized for not advising the other woman as to what was happening. "It was not really a committee matter," she explained. "That is to

say, no committee decisions were called for, and it was
simply a question of carrying out orders from Lon."

"I must have been very unobservant," Koralin admitted. "People going, new people coming, faces changing—I was aware of it but it didn't mean anything.
And the committee members . . ."

"All but one have returned to Lon. The committee
has been disbanded."

"It was through Alph that I learned that he was now
being left completely alone. Nobody had told me."

"I'm sorry about that," Loron said. "The fifteen
thousand new Alphs become more important."

"What is to happen to him?"

"That is yet to be decided. Very soon, I imagine.
Did you make any attempt in the matter we talked
about—further education?"

Koralin smiled ruefully. "Yes. I've been trying, in a
conversational sort of way, but without much success.
He simply rejects as fantasy everything he doesn't already know."

"He's been too well educated already—by experts,"
Loron said with cynicism. "Still, you might as well keep
talking to him, just to break the monotony and prove
there are other human beings about the place. How
is he taking it?"

"It's difficult to say. He tends to be unresponsive,
but I think he knows he is being neglected and feels
he is no longer important. There is suspicion in his
manner—a kind of thoughtful brooding."

"Damn," Loron remarked. "I wish Lon would make
up its mind what the hell it wants done with him.
Meanwhile you'd better try to keep him cheerful. I
imagine you're about the only civilized company he's
got, unless you count the woman who serves his meals
and makes his bed."

"I'll do my best, said Koralin, "but I'd be grateful
if you would let me know as soon as you receive instructions. . . ."

"Don't worry. I will."

That was the end of the short interview, but it left Koralin in a happier frame of mind. She had not been told what was happening to Alphaville, nor did she particularly care, but she had been given what amounted to an open brief to make Alph her personal responsibility during the remainder of his stay. But how long would that be? Weeks, days—or possibly only a few hours? That was a disturbing uncertainty, but at least she could ignore the schedule, which no longer existed, and the attendants, who had gone, and spend the whole day every day with Alph, if she so elected, until time ran out. And that made all the difference in the world.

It had been Koralin's practice during the hot summer days to talk to Alph in the garden or in the woodlands, where they would follow the course of the narrow stream to where it disappeared through a narrow slot in the high smooth wall. She had deliberately not entered his suite or rooms, so that she could not be accused by staff members of intervening in his official supervision and program. In the open they could be observed, at least in theory; among the trees and in the glades of the wood there were secluded places, but she never stayed there long.

But now the rules of the game had changed. That evening she went down into the garden in the usual way to talk to him, but after a while, when he suggested walking to the stream to see the fish, she said: "No. Tonight we shall go to your room instead."

He looked momentarily surprised. "Why? I eat and sleep in my room. You do not usually come there."

"I have seen the fish, but I have not seen your room, so we will go there. Come on, Alph."

After a moment of hesitation, he accepted her instruction. She allowed him to lead the way from the garden, across a paved area, through the double glass door that opened directly into his living quarters.

The entrance hall was quite small, with three plain doors—presumably, living room, bedroom and bathroom. They went into the living room. It was, as expected, functional rather than comfortable, though some attempt had been made to provide a colorful, nursery-like decor. She thought the yellow and green walls clashed with the blue ceiling and the deep red carpet, but perhaps he was not sensitive to the garish rainbow effect. For the rest, the furnishing was standard, though rather below executive class. No books and no pictures, but there was a small videomusic tape player, no doubt designed for entertainment rather than education. And there were shelves bearing boxes of games of diverse kinds, which no doubt he used to play with his attendants at one time, but now that he was alone he didn't seem the type to play solitaire.

"It is a nice room," she commented. "Let's sit down."

They sat on opposite sides of the rectangular table. "You have a better room," he said.

"About the same, but there are not so many colors."

He looked around. "Mm—I like the colors, but sometimes I wish they would change."

"They will, soon. You will be going away from here into new rooms in a new place."

"That is one of your funny stories," he said flatly, without change of expression. "I have been here all my life. There is nowhere else to go."

"Beyond the wall."

He smiled. "Across a blue ocean to a big city with millions of people? You are good at making things up, but I do not believe you."

"One day you will. There are many new people in Alphaville. They are going to tear down the buildings and put up new buildings in their place, and the town will become very much bigger—like one of the cities I have told you about."

"With millions of people, no doubt . . ."

"Not millions, but thousands more. And there will also be new Alphs, many more Alphs—just like you only younger. Small boys, just as you were seven or eight years ago."

He seemed to think the idea ridiculous. "How can there be many more Alphs when I am Alph? How can I be more than one person?"

"They have made more Alphs out of the seeds they took from your body."

"Perhaps they have made more people, but they are not me—they cannot be Alphs, can they?"

That, at least, was logical, and she had to smile. "That is true. They are not you, but they are like you. Their bodies are the same as yours; but your body is not the same as mine, or the bodies of other women like me."

"But we are all women and we are the same. I do not understand you. I am not different."

"You are. For one thing you have hair on your face."

"Ah," he said thoughtfully, stroking the young beard on his chin.

"That is because you are a man. I do not have such hair because I am not a man—I am a woman."

He became impatient. "What is man? I do not understand man—a woman without a 'wo'? They did not tell me about man. You are playing with funny words again."

"I am serious," Koralin insisted. This was the central issue on which the whole of Alph's mental reorientation hinged. It had to succeed, or perhaps fail forever. "When you were very young you were the only man—a baby man—in the world, and all the rest of the people in the world were women. But today there are many thousands of young men and baby men, because the women have made them from your seeds."

He thought about that for quite a long time, as if trying to make sense out of it, and for once he appeared to be reluctant to reject a new idea simply because it was unfamiliar. That, to Koralin's way of thinking, represented a small milestone of progress. The long-deferred lesson was at last beginning to move and take shape, and she sensed a tenseness developing within her at the imminence of what had to be done.

"Why should they do that?" he asked finally. "You say there are millions of people beyond the wall, so why should they want to make more people and call them men?"

"Because there are too many women in the world and not enough men. In order to make people there should be one man for each woman." That was not strictly accurate, of course, even ignoring the technicalities of parthenogenesis, but she was determined to use simple words and ideas that he could understand.

"That is wrong," he said with a sigh. "One person can make people. Why do you say there must be two people? We can all make people."

"Yes, but the seed must grow inside a woman. It grows into a baby. A man cannot grow a baby by himself. So his seed must be put into a woman."

"I do not understand. Women have their own seeds, and they can make their own babies."

"But they can only make woman babies—not man babies. That is why a man's seed must be put inside a woman. It has to join with her seed to make a man baby."

"It all sounds silly to me," he said, looking unhappy. "I think you are making it all up, though I do not know why."

"I am *not* making it up," she said firmly. "I can *prove* that you are a man and I am a woman, and that we are different. And I can show you how a man and a woman make babies the natural way, without tubes and machines."

"How can you prove . . . ?"

She stood up, her heart beating noticeably faster, and leaned across the table, taking his arm. "I think, Alph, that it would be better if we went into your bedroom. . . ."

Chapter Sixteen

It had become evident to Loron over a period of time that certain dramatic changes had taken place in government policies—and quite obvious that rigid censorship had been imposed. The day-to-day communication between Alphaville and Lon were formal and mainly concerned with the reconstruction project that was being planned and evaluated. Because of this the communication channels tended to be monopolized by data transmission, as the architects and engineers on the site made use of the central computer network to speed their calculations. What might be termed general social and political communiqués were noticeably absent, and so far as the public broadcast media were concerned the world was dying of inactivity and boredom. That in itself was a sure sign that momentous events were happening, or about to happen, under a heavy security blanket.

Unlike her predecessor, who had been one of the old "rule-book" guard of technocrats, Loron possessed a keen political instinct. What was not said was only too frequently more significant than what actually *was* said; and there were unofficial sources of information, often unreliable, among the many newcomers to Alphaville, which cast new light from fresh angles on the outside world. Above all, it was now perfectly clear

that the proposed new Alphaville was to be more than
just an expanded center to cope with Phase 3 of the
project. In its final version, so far as she could estimate
in the absence of specific information, it would be at
least ten times larger than required and divided into
two independent zones. New underground works and
buildings were scheduled at points around the perimeter of the island, suggesting defense installations.
Although the amount of construction entailed in the
entire conversion was immense, it was to be started
almost immediately and completed at high speed on
a crash priority basis.

Of one thing Loron could be sure—that whatever
Galinia was up to was also being repeated by the Heads
of State of other countries. Extensive and costly planning on such a vast scale was certain to be the result
of decisions taken internationally, and she knew that
there had been several sessions of the Central World
Advisory Council on Technology and Administration
in recent months. All of the sessions had been secret.

She thought about the situation very carefully, trying to fit the known facts and rumors into a sensible
pattern, like pieces into a hypothetical jigsaw puzzle,
until she thought she could see the overall picture, or
perhaps several alternative pictures. Then, being a
woman of action, diplomatic action, as well as a thinker,
she sent a confidential communication addressed personally to Galinia, Head of State in Lon, tendering her
resignation as administrative chief of the Alphaville
center.

As she had anticipated, the response from Lon was
immediate. She was peremptorily summoned to present
herself in person and without delay before the Head
of State to explain her unprecedented action. With a
quiet smile of satisfaction she called her secretary and
instructed her to charter a special flight to deliver her
to Lon that same day, book a suite in the best available hotel, and notify the Head of State that she would

be at her disposal from 10 o'clock the next morning.

Meanwhile, Galinia sat comfortably installed in her circular office at the summit of the Silver Tower in Lon like an eagle in its aerie, although she did not feel in the least like a bird of prey. Before her on the desk was the confidential dossier on Loron. She had met the woman before on several occasions, but could only recall that she was attractive and personable, with plenty of self-possession backed by an unobtrusive air of authority.

According to the terse details in the dossier, Loron was thirty-eight years of age, educated in America and Europe, with a brilliant record of academic and scientific achievements in the service of the State; she was politically neutral, security clear, with a Keisintel factor that just brought her into the eugenic Alpha category, though rather too late in life for practical applications. Loron herself would not be aware of her eugenic rating —until the Alph program began, such information was known only to the genetic scientists. It did, however, give her a specific qualification, which Galinia noted in her mind.

As to why she had been appointed to the responsible Alphaville post in succession to the late Davana, the dossier reported enigmatically: "Selected for compatible interface, analytical ability, and unorthodox approach to problem solving; sound organizer with political flair in decision making." That seemed to pose a number of unanswered questions. A footnote at the end added: "History of success in originating and handling new projects, but inclined to be impatient. This should correct itself with advancing age and responsibility. Likes to be fully committed to new or non-routine work."

"Why, then, the resignation?" Galinia asked herself, speaking aloud as if expecting a disembodied voice to answer. The amended Phase 3 of Project Alpha was certainly new and challenging, and guaranteed to keep any executive at full stretch for years to come. Of course, Loron didn't know much about it yet, and could not be aware of the major changes in policy that had been agreed on internationally, but she must have had the sense to realize from her own observations and inevitable rumors that something really big was about to happen at a speed that should more than satisfy her alleged impatience. Well, she would know soon enough tomorrow.

She closed the dossier and put it in a drawer, then opened the latest security intelligence file on her desk. The contents made depressing reading to a woman of charitable nature acting under uncharitable international pressures. Further arrests among the more vociferous of the lunatic anti-Keisintel faction, more deaths among young eugenic Alpha women—two of them suicides and the rest suspected murders, or perhaps assassination would be the better word—and another bomb explosion at the Partho-8 center, despite the stringent security precautions. Riots and demonstrations against official attempts to control and curb the decadent practice of simulo by enforced psycho-reorientation in special State clinics. And a massive list of "suspects" detained for truth-drug interrogation on a hit-or-miss random selection principle. On the average, about one person in twenty made an admission of some sort that could be followed up by the security forces and police.

It seemed to Galinia that the world was falling apart at a time when it should be consolidating its progress in the light of new freedoms and new philosophies, but on the available evidence something had gone seriously wrong with both the freedoms and the philosophies. At the recent International Council meetings there had, predictably, been as many opinions as there had been delegates and Heads of States, so that final decisions, made by ballot, were invariably a compromise between action and inaction; but in general the agreed-on policies favored reaction, in its political sense, which seemed to her to be the wrong kind of reversionism

and merely a holding maneuver while the details of
some kind of fundamental reform were hammered out.

And that meant the full paraphernalia of internal
security—government by decree and arrest without war-
rant under emergency regulations, while behind the
scenes new plans were being drawn up to continue a
modified Alpha program under conditions of increasing social disaffection. It involved more than enough
administrative work in itself without having to be ac-
commodating to a resignation-tendering executive, however important, who no doubt only wished to air some
minor parochial complaints. Loron, she suspected, was
merely impatient to learn what was *really* going to
happen in Alphaville, and she was no doubt anxious to
get Alph off her hands, now that he had been discarded.

She closed the security file and put it away with the
ironic realization that, if it came to the point, political
affiliations apart, she would probably be much happier
leading the rebels than suppressing them, for she had
once been a rebel herself, and the feeling died hard.

Loron arrived at the Silver Tower at precisely the appointed time to find Galinia sitting behind a totally
empty desk, which indicated that all documents and
files had been put away. On the control panel of the
desk minute red and green lights gleamed. Loron, who
knew about control panels, recognized that full audio
and video recording had been switched on. Well, it
was nice to know that one was speaking for the archives.

Galinia was the acme of courtesy. She came around
the desk to usher Loron into a seat, and poured her a
drink without asking. Then, characteristically, she came
straight to the point.

"A resignation at your administrative level is invariably a political maneuver," she said. "Therefore I suggest we take the maneuver as read and get down to the underlying motivation."

Loron smiled. "You credit me with more subtlety than I possess, Mistress. But since you mention motivation, perhaps we could come directly to the subject of Alphaville and the changes that are being put in hand—with almost indecent haste. I should be interested in the motivation behind all that."

"So should we all," Galinia said. "We each of us see international policies being implemented at our own particular levels, and we must form our own interpretations. Even so, I cannot see that the decision to enlarge and redesign Alphaville should be a cause for anxiety. The entire Alpha project is beginning to assume vast proportions, including a number of ramifications that were not foreseen."

Loron considered her words carefully. "It is the ramifications that concern me. But even if we consider only the facts as they exist, it is perfectly clear that the proposed new Alphaville is going to be at least ten times larger than required—which surely is far more than necessary to cope with Phase 3 of the project. Presumably, the same degree of overextension is being carried out at Alpha centers in other countries. After all, Mistress, you did mention international policies."

"I think we are merely looking ahead," Galinia said in a matter-of-fact voice. "It would be uneconomic to undertake new expansions and reconstructions every fifteen years or so."

"Why the fortifications?"

Galinia's eyes seemed to frost over a little. "What fortifications?"

"Perhaps I am mistaken. I had an impression that the smaller structures around the perimeter of the island looked somewhat military—or perhaps defensive would be the better word—in the planning stage. There's a great deal of excavating going on."

"Well," said Galinia, "I am not an architect, nor am I a computer. No doubt there is a method in what may appear to be madness. Sites for power stations, telecommunications, radar and that kind of thing, perhaps. One can never be sure what the scientists and engineers are up to these days."

"As Head of State it's your job to be sure," Loron stated flatly. The atmosphere in the room changed instantly. Galinia's matronly and rather patronizing cordiality switched itself off, leaving a cold, formal figurehead. But there was no hostility—not even a hint of disapproval at the other woman's critical tone of voice.

"Tell me, Loron," Galinia said after a pause, "precisely *why* did you resign? Surely it was not because you felt that the new Alphaville would be too big and complex for you to administer."

"Not at all, Mistress. But I have no desire to be the commander of a fortress under siege—which is the way I evaluate the situation."

"Would you care to explain what you mean by that incredible statement?"

"Certainly, provided you will guarantee my freedom and grant that what I say is privileged."

"I am not above the law."

"But you are Head of State. In any case, I have nothing seditious to say—indeed, nothing to say that could not be deduced by any intelligent observer of the scene, given certain information."

"Then you need neither guarantee nor privilege."

"Very well, Mistress. In that case I shall explain to you the reasoning behind what you regard as my extraordinary statement."

Loron explained.

Starting with the fact of the unexpected escalation of the Phase 3 reconstruction of Alphaville, there was one thing of which she could be sure: that whatever Galinia was up to was also being implemented by the Heads of State of other countries. Extensive and costly planning on such a scale was bound to be the result of decisions taken internationally, and she knew that there had been several sessions of the Central World Advisory Council on Technology and Administration in recent months. All of the sessions had been secret.

It was not so difficult to add up some of the integers to provide a guide number to the total score. First, one had to start with reversionism itself, the more liberal pattern of government that had demolished the rigid totalitarianism of the previous regime and exposed the perverse sexual mythology founded on an enforced Lesbian and parthenogenetic function—the discredited syndrome. So far so good; if the people were still not free, at least they were freer than could reasonably have been foreseen before the revolution. But political freedom was not, in fact, the fundamental driving force of reversionism. What mattered above all was the promise—the dream—of biological freedom, of the ultimate return to a normal bisexual community, even though it was a concept which few women of the day could comprehend in real terms.

Reversionary governments, inexperienced in such matters, reasonably supposed that by a process of education the existing monosexual syndrome would gradually diminish and dissolve, leaving a vacuum of nonpracticing heterosexuality as an interim stage. In due course steps would officially be taken to "train" women in the new behavior patterns intrinsic to a society of males and females. And, thanks to accidental but nevertheless perfect timing, the whole dramatic change could be effected in such a way as to make the best possible use of the Keisintel principles, so that the expanding nucleus of the magnificent new heterosexual humanity of the future would be as eugenically perfect as science could make it. That was the package of goodies for which the grateful female sex would, it was supposed, offer eternal thanks to their wise and benevolent reversionist leaders.

All noble planning; but how was the scheme shaping up after some seventeen years of reversionist administration? The male child was now a young man who, by artificial insemination, had fathered more than fifteen thousand sons. But he did not know he was a man, or even what "man" meant, and he was eugenically substandard by Keisintel's rules. Furthermore, his gametes were no longer required, and the administration so far had no idea what to do with him—nor, apparently, had they any idea of what they proposed to do with the fifteen thousand first-generation substandard males when they eventually reached their father's redundancy age. The truth was that they were simply laboratory breeding stock and in no way a part of living society.

What about the mothers? Ah, there the Keisintel schematic was in full swing. From the young female adults of the world the eugenic best had been creamed off to conceive and bear and improve the male stock. These selected and privileged young women were the selfless pioneers of the most magnificent experiment in all history. And in subsequent generations of breeding their places would be taken by even more eugenically refined mothers. Keisintel couldn't lose—the computers would see to that.

And at the end of the game, when all the breeding and selection and refining had been accomplished, then the perfect males and the perfect females could be trained to live together in a state of ecstatic mutual symbiosis, to multiply and be fruitful until, in the course of time, the substandard hordes had died their natural deaths, leaving Homo sapiens as a superb race of gods and goddesses, with the ghost of the long-dead Keisintel no doubt smiling gratified approval from that other dark dimension.

That was the beautiful theory; but so far as the here and now were concerned, you could forget about the coming heterosexual utopia. You could forget about it for a hundred years, and probably much longer. That left the reality of Alph and his little Alphs segregated behind stringent security barriers, and the eugenic Alpha females, as the selected mothers were known, whose Keisintel-style perfection had been deemed suitable for forward propagation to populate the glittering world of the distant future.

What else remained? Why, only the vast mass of more than one thousand million women who were regarded as genetically substandard because the DNA protein code in the chromosomes of their cells did not conform to Keisintel's specification. They had no role to play in the great experiment other than to continue to provide routine parthenogenetic females for the eugenic scientists to work on in their laboratories. But for them, also, the male child was a symbol of aspiration; and they too were involved in the slow dissolution of the Lesbian syndrome as it crumbled like an outmoded religion. But they were the rejected—the subspecies condemned to ultimate extinction.

Here, then, existed a political incubator for stress and conflict. From it would emerge avant-garde pressures for reform and change, not from a minority but, as the movement spread, from the majority of womankind. Since change in human affairs tends to happen swiftly and unexpectedly, there would be sudden outbreaks of behavior patterns inimical to convention and social stability, and an increasing clamor for equality and the abolition of privilege in the long-term eugenic plan. And that meant an anti-Keisintel and therefore anti-government movement, and logically the hostility would be focused upon the selected eugenic Alpha females, because they were symbols of the new superior class and therefore constituted a threat to the majority.

Inevitably there would be a sharp reaction by authority—increased security, a return to totalitarian administration, greater protective segregation of the males and also the Alpha females, not forgetting the scientific staff concerned in the project. There would be censorship and control of communications to retard the spread of subversive ideologies. Finally, as a precautionary contingency measure, would come the establishment of vast maximum security zones to house and defend the Alpha males and females and their scientific retinue, in which the eugenic program could continue, divorced from the restless mass of nonparticipating humanity.

All this was more than mere speculation on Loron's part. It was a perceptive attempt to take the situation as it existed, reduce it to its basic operating premises and parameters, predict the counterforces that would arise to control dissident forces breaking through established restraints, and build up, as it were, a model of such a world in action, taking into account the hypothetical mainsprings of human behavior. Such fragments of hard fact as she possessed fitted neatly into the theoretical pattern of the jigsaw puzzle. Now what mattered was Galinia's response.

But Galinia was not making any immediate response. Her eyes were cool and reflective, as if she were trying to recall a half-forgotten word on the tip of her tongue, and with one elbow on the desk, she was supporting her chin gently with the tip of her forefinger. Although her eyes were directed towards Loron, they appeared to be looking through her at some point beyond. Loron said nothing further—she knew that she had already said more than enough.

Presently Galinia took her finger from her chin and pointed it at Loron.

"And then?"

Loron shrugged her shoulders. "I have made my analysis, but it is not for me to gaze into crystal balls. If you would like me to forecast a new world insurrection between the Keisintelites and the anti-Keisintelites, then I must disappoint you, Mistress."

"And which faction would win such a conflict?" Galinia asked, ignoring Loron's evasiveness.

"It depends what you mean by 'win,' Mistress. I suppose one can win by putting all Alpha men and women into impregnable fortresses and simply waiting for the enemy to die a natural death, but it will take a long time, and there will be serious problems of logistics and supplies between the many national fortresses. On the other hand, if sheer numbers count for anything . . ."

"And how would *you* resolve such a situation, Loron?"

"I am not a politician, Mistress. It is for you to answer such a question. All I have put to you is the proposition that, if you create a small sub-society of the eugenically heterosexual elite within a mass monosexual society of the discarded non-elite, then you have erected a terrifying class—indeed, racial—barrier, which must be torn down sooner or later."

"It cannot be torn down while the Keisintel eugenic laws still exist," Galinia said firmly.

"That is precisely my point, Mistress."

Galinia drew in a slow, deep breath. "Abandon Keisintel?"

"The new men do not belong to the scientists. Nor do women. They belong to each other."

"And the super-race?"

"Designed and specified by the long-dead Keisintel with the aid of computers. Perhaps in a monosexual parthenogenetic female world there may be a case for selective breeding, as there is no mechanism for random genetic variation. But with the advent of the new men . . ."

Galinia stood up and regarded the other woman in a melancholy fashion. Her voice when she spoke was not unsympathetic. "It's a fascinating theory, Loron, and I have no doubt you feel better for having aired it. Let's have another drink before you depart."

She refilled the glasses and continued: "You must not confuse theory with facts. Whatever the future may hold, the Alphavilles of the world will continue to be the nursery of the new male sex, and will call for our best scientists and administrators. I am afraid I cannot accept your resignation."

"But if I insist, Mistress. . .?"

Galinia moved her head and at the same time winked. Loron was absolutely positive about the wink. It had been marginal and fractional, and partly disguised by the head movement, probably to foil the monitoring video cameras. Apart from the wink itself, there was nothing in Galinia's bland expression to hint at any kind of secret or withheld communication.

"Do not insist now," Galinia said. "Go back to your hotel and reflect on it. Rest for a day or two. I shall contact you again and we can have a further discussion. Things are not nearly so complex as you imagine."

Loron accepted the compromise with good grace. In view of the unexpected wink there was little else she could do. But as she returned to the hotel her mind was spinning along new political trajectories.

Chapter Seventeen

Alph's introduction to the ways of a man with a maid at the hands of Koralin had, conversely, also been Koralin's introduction in practical terms to the ways of a maid with a man. That first occasion had been for her a wildly exciting and miserably disappointing experience. The mere act of showing him her naked body and pointing out its delicate functional intricacies had set her afire with sensual expectancy, but Alph's response was one of perplexity and suspicion, even of mild revulsion, as if he thought she had suffered a nasty accident but was too polite to mention it. And when, after some persuasion, he had removed his clothes, she observed a disheartening absence of physical libido. Her efforts to arouse him, based on academic theory, proved futile; he had been too well-conditioned to respond to the glittering instruments and tubes manipulated by sexless white-coated attendants.

She let the impasse go by default and spent more than an hour talking to him in quiet reassuring tones, explaining the reasons for the differences in the shapes of their bodies, and pointing out that the size of her breasts had nothing to do with overeating, and equally that the streamlined shape of her pubis was not the result of an amputation. Alph remained morose and unconvinced. Koralin, for her part, was no longer con-

cerned with educating Alph for his own good; she had
an urgent physical need of him, and she found it frustrating and shaming to be confronted with indifference
and impotence.

The situation was too tense and unfamiliar, she
realized when she paused to think about it rationally.
For one thing, Alph was unaccustomed to having a
woman in his own private bedroom, and for another,
he needed time to assimilate and adapt to the undeni-
able visual and tactile evidence of masculinity and
femininity. So they dressed again, and she suggested
that they walk in the garden as far as the stream.

It was there, in the familiar woodland surroundings,
that she eventually achieved her object. Even so, it was
not without its difficulties of communication. When,
after persistent and patient caressing, she finally succeeded in arousing a virile physical reaction, he assumed
that she merely wished to take a sample of seed, though
in a most unusual way and without the use of instruments. All her careful explanations had failed to make
any impression.

"No," she breathed, trying to suppress her impatience, "I do not want to take a sample. You must put
your seed inside me. Here . . ." She took his hand to
guide him.

"But that is not natural. . . ."

"It *is* natural, Alph. You must try. Come nearer."

"It is not comfortable."

She adjusted the position of her body. "There
now . . ."

"That is better. What do I do now?"

"You must move, like so . . ."

Alph moved for a while, very tentatively, holding
her slackly around the waist. Suddenly his grip tightened
and the whirlwind struck, seizing control of his body
from his own conscious volition. Koralin, who had been
poised for so long on the brink of delirium, was immediately caught up in the incandescent fire of orgasm,

and she had relaxed, almost comatose, long before he had finished his violent thrusting invasion of her body. And then he too subsided and detached himself from her.

Gently she stroked his long hair and his softly bearded face "Well, Alph—did you like it?" she asked.

He considered for a while. "I do not know," he said, still gasping for breath. "It is a very difficult way of giving seed."

"It is the best way of all," she murmured.

After that initiation ceremony, tortuous though it had been, there was no restraining Alph. For that matter, there was no restraining Koralin, either. And behind her sheer physical satiation was the exultant knowledge that she was the only woman in the entire world—the only woman in five centuries—to have been made love to by a man. A young man, admittedly, little more than a youth, but still a genuine male specimen of Homo sapiens. For days she wandered around as if in a dreamworld, in a perpetual state of obsessive excitement, and it was gratifying to find Alph waiting hungrily and lustfully for her every time she visited him. For a while, during this phase of mutual physical infatuation, the education program, such as it was, came to a halt, although in a sense they were educating each other in a new kind of experience.

Naturally, Koralin kept her new relationship with Alph secret. Precisely why she felt it necessary to do this was difficult for her to analyze. Loron would almost certainly disapprove, of that she felt certain, even though Alph had been discarded as a source of gametes. True, Loron had gone off to Lon on a confidential mission to see Galinia, the Head of State, so that there was no immediate danger of discovery and possible disciplinary action. Perhaps what she feared most was being sent away from Alphaville to separate her from the first man—that was not quite unthinkable. Already she had become possessive and—though she could not identify the unaccustomed feeling—jealous that he should occasionally come into contact with other women. Alph was hers, and nobody else must know.

Alph, on the other hand, was possessive in quite a different way. Since the termination of his function as a donor of gametes he had been largely isolated and neglected. The sudden and remarkable discovery that putting seed samples into the living body of Koralin was an incredibly more exhilarating and pleasurable function than delivering up to the demanding tubes and instruments made him determined that he should not lose her—more, that he should use her for that purpose at every possible opportunity.

But Koralin had also explained to him that she was physically and functionally the same as all other women. This was difficult for him to accept, for other women were remote and impersonal beings, and quite neutral insofar as this new concept of sex was concerned. The idea lay dormant in the depths of his simple mind, but whenever he was examined by a medico, or the woman came to tidy his room and bring him his meals, he would eye them with veiled interest, trying to visualize Koralin's body beneath the skirts and capes.

It happened within a few days, while Loron was still away in Lon. One morning his breakfast was brought to him by a young woman he had not seen before. She was slender and attractive, with long curved legs that drew his gaze much more than did those of Koralin, and the hanging folds of her cape implied that the territory beneath was more ambitiously protuberant. His heart beat a little faster, and the familiar electricity tingled in his pelvis. Her manner was formal, as was the case with all the women, and she hardly bothered to glance at him at all as she delivered the trolley to his room.

He ate in a desultory fashion, pondering in his mind this strange exercise called sex, and wondering why it had not been explained to him many years earlier. After breakfast he waited for her to return to remove the trolley. There was no plan in his mind, but merely an urge to discover if she was like Koralin.

And indeed she was. Her scream as he seized her startled him, but he retained his grip on her arms. "Do not be afraid," he said, pushing her towards the bedroom. "I will not hurt you." She stared at him wide-eyed in a kind of horrified fascination, but she did not scream again. Nobody came to her rescue, and quite soon she had no wish to be rescued. She was a young woman who had had previous experience of simulo, and now she was being confronted for the first time in her life with the reality; but it was not without some trepidation that she allowed Alph to have his way with her. Anxiety inhibited her own responses, so that it was all over before her own growing excitement could reach a climactic level, but she was glad to escape in order to think over this strange and unexpected assault.

"You were good," Alph said appreciatively. "You were much better than Koralin."

"Thank you," she replied as she wheeled the breakfast trolley from the room.

The mention of Koralin's name cast the incident into a quite different perspective. The thing that had initially puzzled her—Alph's facile expertise—was now explained. She wondered whether Koralin had been officially authorized to train the male in the mechanics of what she regarded as real-life simulo; but even so, the sexual attack on herself was totally without permission or sanction. Not that it had been so unpleasant, when it came to the point, but where would it stop? Did Alph consider that he now had free access to any member of the Alphaville staff who came within his orbit? Well, perhaps he had, but it was necessary to find out.

As Loron was still away, later in the day she went to see her secretary, the oriental young woman who had continued to hold arrogant power since the regime of Davana. The secretary, whose name was Sharn, listened impassively to the sensational recitation of Alph's misdemeanor, and made a mental note of the name Koralin, whom she recalled as a rather neurotic and occasionally troublesome supernumerary who had no useful function at Alphaville.

"I shall send a report to Lon," Sharn said. "Meanwhile I shall remove you from attendant duties on the Alpha male and suspend Koralin pending a formal investigation."

"Oh," said the young woman. "I am quite prepared to continue with my duties. It's not as if he injured me in any way. It just seemed—well, a little irregular, and I thought perhaps I ought to report it."

"You were quite correct to do so. The incident is most irregular, and I am certain that Loron will take the most decisive measures to make sure that it cannot possibly occur again. As for Koralin—her part in the matter calls for an inquiry at the highest level."

And that was that, but the victim of Alph's innocent act of rape was beginning to wish she had kept silent about the matter. However, it was now too late; the news was out, and she saw no reason why she should not also tell her friends about her thrilling ordeal at the hands of an impassioned Alph. Simulo had nothing on the real thing. Why was Alph being wasted by being kept a virtual prisoner? Why should Koralin be the only woman allowed free access to him and his remarkable talents? In other words, where had this new dynamic Alph been all their lives?

The young woman's story was received with various reactions ranging from horror through circumspection to curious envy. And while Loron was still detained on government business in Lon, the situation hung fire. As for Koralin, her first intimation that anything dramatic had happened was the receipt of a peremptory summons from secretary Sharn.

Sharn, adopting her most inscrutable and impersonal pose, was determined to make the most of her opportunity to humiliate the woman who had bypassed her on a number of occasions in order to waste the time of her busy superiors—the late Davana in particular. She did not ask Koralin to sit down, but Koralin, who anticipated trouble, would have preferred to stand anyway.

"A matter of some importance has come to my attention," Sharn said in a quiet bored voice, as though the whole thing were too tedious for words. "It concerns the relationship between yourself and the Alpha male."

Koralin, to her credit, remained totally impassive.

"In the temporary absence of the administrative head of Alphaville," Sharn continued, "I am placing the Alpha male in total isolation. Special arrangements will be made for catering and other essential services under conditions of security. All association between yourself and the Alpha male will cease as of now. That is a directive."

Now panic was beginning to flutter inside her, but she kept it firmly suppressed. Under no circumstances would she permit herself to show signs of weakness or apprehension in front of the hated Sharn.

Koralin said: "You have no authority to issue a directive of any kind. The limit of your responsibility is to refer the matter to Loron and await instructions."

"That will be done as soon as the telecommunication channels are clear. Meanwhile I must ask you to remain in your quarters. I have the delegated responsibility to requisition the use of force, if necessary."

"Not on me you haven't," Koralin said. "I am not a

member of the staff: I am here at the discretion of the
Head of State, to whom I am directly responsible. So
be careful, Sharn. Be very careful."

That was not strictly true, of course, but it was
enough to baffle the secretary for a few moments, long
enough to allow Koralin to make a dignified exit. In the
corridor, however, her poise broke down. A thousand
questioning anxieties pierced her mind like probing
needles. How could Sharn have found out? Who had
been spying and talking? Alph himself, perhaps, but
she had stressed the need for secrecy. And yet, with
his simple mind, one accidental word . . .

She hurried, almost ran, along the passages and down
the steps that led to Alph's special accommodation
unit, aware that other women were watching her with
inquisitive eyes. They all knew, she was sure of that.
The panic leaped to a higher level of urgency. She
hated herself for her lack of self-control, but this was
a crisis that threatened her future existence at Alphaville and could even jeopardize the fate of Alph himself. She had to be calm and rational and work things
out before Loron returned, but first she must know the
truth.

There was no immediate sign of Alph in the visible
part of the garden. He might be in the woods by the
stream, but first she went into his apartment. The
living rooms were empty. It did not occur to her that
he could be in his bedroom in the middle of a sunny
afternoon, and she was about to make for the distant
stream when the sound of voices stopped her dead and
froze her heart. A woman's quiet voice followed by a
laugh, and then the deeper familiar intonation of the
voice of Alph.

She did nothing for a moment, her mind curiously
blank, and then, quite suddenly, everything became
only too clear, and she was astonished that she should
have been so foolish and obsessed as to have overlooked the obvious. The bedroom door was painted

yellow, and a fly crawled diagonally across it from the top right-hand corner. She stared at the fly as if she had never seen one before, but her mind was far away, buried in some dark inner space. Again the voice of Alph and the murmuring of the woman, but the words were not intelligible.

She took one step towards the bedroom door, then stopped. I created him, she told herself. He belongs to me. I risked my life so that he should have his life; therefore his life belongs to me. He has not the right to share it with others.

She stood irresolute, unable to make a decision, her emotions balanced on the knife-edge between anger and despair. Presently the talking ceased and gave way to the sounds of movement and heavy breathing. She clenched her fists until her long nails pierced the palms of her hands, watching without feeling as a trickle of blood ran between her fingers.

And then the conflict within her resolved itself. She sagged visibly as the tension drained from her. What did it matter? she thought. At least she had been the first—perhaps the first of many, for Alph would be bemused with his new-found diversion until authority applied the veto. There would be many women willing to sample the experience that was destined to be the lot of all womankind—at least, that privileged class of womankind conforming to the required eugenic criteria. But she had still been the first, Keisintel-plus or not.

She walked slowly from the apartment and across the garden to the wood and the stream. There, sitting on the grassy bank, she allowed her bloodstained hands to trail in the clear water. Poor Alph, she thought. To live like an animal in a cage. And even now, despite what I taught him, he still does not know what life is all about. I'm not even sure I do myself. I was wrong —he does not belong to me. He does not even belong to himself, and the same fate will await his sons.

Later, in a thoughtful and disconsolate mood, she

returned to her rooms to find a tall matronly woman waiting for her. Koralin merely glanced at her, said nothing, and sat down wearily in a chair near the window.

"I am to share your room for a few days, until Loron returns," the woman said. Her manner was uneasy and apologetic.

Koralin shrugged. "And follow me around and keep me under observation, no doubt."

"Well, not exactly . . ."

"It's all right. Sharn is exceeding her authority, but it doesn't matter. Make yourself at home."

As an afterthought, Koralin asked: "Do you play cards?"

"Yes," said the woman.

"Thank heaven for that. It will make a change from playing solitaire."

Chapter Eighteen

Loron stayed eight days in Lon. During the first complete week, somewhat to her surprise, she received no further communication from Galinia, nor was it possible to make contact with Alphaville. The telecommunication channels were fully loaded with priority data transmissions, they said. It became apparent after the first few days that the absence of communication was deliberate; they were holding her in an information vacuum while deliberations as to her future proceeded at a high governmental and possibly international level.

She was not isolated, however. She could telephone old friends and acquaintances that she knew in Lon, and she took the opportunity to visit some of them. Their manner was cordial but, she thought, constrained. Naturally they regarded her as a high ranking government official with direct access to the Head of State, and possibly for that reason they seemed disinclined to talk about anything that was not trivial and superficial.

Except Rowana—dear drunken drugged Rowana—a former colleague and lover, with whom she had lived for some years in America when both of them were much younger. What Rowana was doing in Lon was not quite clear to Loron; her work seemed to be connected with the documentation of air freight from across the Atlantic, though whether she was ever clear-headed enough to be able to read the documents concerned was doubtful. However, she lived in a comfortable flat in west Lon and appeared to be well able to maintain herself in a semi-luxurious fashion.

Being a woman of some attraction and considerable vivacity, Rowana insisted on celebrating the unexpected reunion with her friend by getting high on ambrosia—which Loron sampled too—and insisting on a passionate bout of Lesbian love-making. Loron complied with some amusement and genuine pleasure; it had been a long time since she had been able to unwind herself in the most fundamental of human relations. At least it proved she was still normal, in the contemporary sense of the word.

But Rowana herself was more versatile. In the late evening she suggested a visit to a club—"a special club," she said with a drunken leer. "You like simulo, don't you?"

"It's illegal," Loron pointed out.

"Oh, come off your government pedestal for a few hours. Every damn thing is illegal these days. It's getting so that it will be much simpler for the State to arrest the few people left who aren't breaking the law."

"I haven't seen much sign of lawlessness."

"It's everywhere. Those uniforms in the streets, and the patrol cars. They practically drive in convoy. And those monitor cameras at the top of the lamp standards."

She pointed an unsteady finger at Loron. "Whenever you see the signs of law enforcement you see lawlessness. The two go together, only one's on the surface and the other is underground. Why do you suppose the countryside is dotted with concentration camps? And why do you suppose the so-called Partho centers have been fortified to protect the Alpha females? You've been missing all the fun, Loron darling."

"So it would seem," Loron agreed.

"Heard any good explosions lately?"

"Yes." She had been awakened in the hotel by a series of concussions in the pre-dawn hours.

"That's the AK Army at work. They seldom miss a night."

Loron did not bother to ask the obvious question. The letters AK clearly stood for anti-Keisintel. It seemed important to her that she should not appear too ignorant if she was to draw further information from Rowana.

"Urban guerilla tactics," she remarked, as if it were of no consequence. "It's all noise and no impact. I haven't noticed the government trembling with fear."

"No—but the Alpha females are. Destroy those and you wipe out Keisintel. It's back to square one in eugenics."

"Killing the Alpha females won't repeal the Keisintel laws," Loron pointed out. "Wouldn't it make more sense to kill the administration and set up a new kind of reversionism?"

Rowana uttered a mock laugh. "Nothing to it—but the females make an easier target." Her mood became serious, almost gloomy. "So there's only one thing to do for someone like me who doesn't want to get involved, and that's to go on the drink and drug kick and play with the perversions."

"That way you'll get involved, too—on the wrong side of the barbed wire," Loron observed. She decided that Rowana was exaggerating in a mood of ambrosia and drug-induced fantasy, but even so . . .

"How do you know all this? The way you talk, Rowana, anyone would think you were a lieutenant in the AK Army instead of a respectable airline official."

"Friends," Rowana said dreamily. "The wrong kind of friends, perhaps, but nice friends. Exciting friends. I like exciting people." She linked her arm with

Loron's. "Let's go on to the club, anyway. I'll introduce you to some of them."

"Another time," Loron said firmly, "when I fancy
some exciting people. Right now I'm worn out."

She returned to the hotel on foot—quite an unusual
thing to do in the deserted streets at that time of
night. The patrols were noticeable, of course, as Rowana had said, but they paid no attention to her. It was
quite likely that the visible presence of so many uniforms was intended as a psychological deterrent. It was
too bad about Rowana, if she was genuinely hooked
on the decadent way of life, though one could not over-
look the possibility that she was part of the establishment, briefed by security to feed certain information to
Loron herself in order to test her reactions. Why else
should Galinia leave her in isolation in Lon, cut off
from Alphaville, for so long? Logically, she could be
expected to fill in the time by seeking out old friends
and colleagues, and one had to bear in mind the possibility that they had already been sought out by Galinia's Intelligence Service to carry out prescribed tasks,
however harmless they might seem. In the highly motivated world of today, it paid to be a cynic.

Among the few further contacts she made during
the remainder of the week there was only one circumspect reference to the AK Army, and this was made
by a young woman who, in fact, worked in the records
branch of Security. "It's made up of a hard core of
militants, but we know who most of them are," she
explained. "They're not rebels in the ordinary sense—
that is, they're not particularly trying to bring down
the government. They know they couldn't win, anyway.
The idea is to force the abolition of the Keisintel class-
division by violence—bombing Partho centers and
laboratories, destroying genetic records, and by assassination and murder of Alpha-plus women and eugenic
scientists."

"Why don't you arrest them?" Loron asked.

"We do, from time to time, but it's better psychology to let them run free and arrest their recruits. After all, they don't do the dirty work themselves if they can avoid it. Rebel leaders seldom do. They get their army from the growing mass of addicts—drugs and simulo. In fact, they're the addiction pushers for the most part. But we've got the situation well under control, and we can pull them in as and when we choose."

Nevertheless, Loron thought, the AK Army as a subversive movement had one thing going for it which could make for success—a strongly emotional cause based on a class and privilege struggle. In that sense it was not political, and therefore it had the potential dynamism to win. What was under attack was not the administration but the whole concept of selective breeding of the human species. Keisintel as a god was under fire from the eugenic atheists.

On the morning of the eighth day Loron received a written message, delivered by hand, summoning her to the Silver Tower for a further interview with the Head of State. It marked a welcome end to a period of frustrating uncertainty, not to mention a week of relative inactivity during which she had more than enough time to rethink her attitudes. Not that there had been any change of mind; she was convinced that her basic arguments were still valid.

Galinia seemed in a genial mood. On this occasion a number of papers were strewn on her desk and most of the monitor lights on the control unit were out, which suggested an informal session—though not necessarily off the record. A seat, a drink and a half minute of unimportant chat about the hotel, the weather, and Lon in general.

Then Galinia said: "I must apologize for not having

contacted you sooner, my dear Loron, but there have been a number of important policy meetings which proved time-consuming. Also, it was necessary to discuss your case at World Advisory Council level."

"I assumed as much," Loron said.

"I am advised to accept your resignation."

Loron said nothing. She sat holding the glass in her hand, rotating it slowly with her fingers.

"Naturally I am very sorry," Galinia went on. "Indeed, we are all very sorry—but you must be allowed to make your own decision, free from political pressure."

"I understand, Mistress."

"You will also understand that, as all governments are committed to enforcement of the Keisintel laws—for the present, anyway—we cannot endorse a senior administrator holding opposite views."

"I don't recall stating any opposite views," Loron said carefully. "I merely analyzed what I thought to be the current situation and thought that it might lead to conflict over the implementation of the Keisintel principles."

"That is already happening, and one must decide where one's allegiance lies. In any event, it is the duty of the State to protect its citizens from deliberate politically motivated murder—or do you feel that the Alpha females should be sacrificed in the interests of eugenic freedom?"

"The State must maintain law and order," Loron agreed, "but I see nothing wrong with the principle of eugenic freedom."

"Even if it has to be achieved by violent insurrection."

"We used the method ourselves only seventeen years ago," Loron pointed out.

Galinia picked up a piece of paper from the desk. "We have not yet appointed your successor, which is a pity. There's trouble at Alphaville. The Alpha male, according to a communiqué from your secretary—or rather your former secretary—has been enthusiastically impregnating every female he has been able to lay his hands on, and most of them seem to have enjoyed the experience. I have no doubt that it is an improvement on simulo, which, according to intelligence reports, is also practiced secretly at Alphaville, as you probably know."

"I know," said Loron, sitting stiff and taut in her chair, "but why wasn't I informed of the other matter?"

Galinia spread out her hands. "Why should you be? You had tendered your resignation. All communications from Alphaville were intercepted."

"But Alph—he knew nothing of heterosex. Why should he suddenly go berserk like—well, like an animal?"

"He did not go berserk. His amusing little trick was taught to him by none other than Koralin—in a sense his creator. There is a kind of incestuous justice about it. Apparently it was part of an unofficial educational program which you, personally, had approved and authorized."

"Oh," Loron said, taken aback. "The facts are not quite like that, but I am not abdicating responsibility. There was a problem in keeping both Koralin and the Alpha male occupied and free from boredom. . . ."

"You succeeded admirably," Galinia said, not without a trace of humor in her voice. "Indeed, you have succeeded in introducing non-Keisintel heterosexual relations into the world several generations before even the first Keisintel copulations were envisaged. You may even have changed the course of history, Loron."

Loron recovered some of her poise. There was no discernible threat in Galinia's manner; if anything, a subtle question was being posed, though she was unable to guess at its nature.

"What will happen now—to Alph, to Koralin?"

"What indeed? It is a local matter and can be dealt with locally by the new administrator. Alph is unimportant, and heterosexual activity has to start somewhere, sometime. There need be no conceptions. Our abortifacients are very efficient."

She paused, eyeing Loron with a weary air. "Candidly, the World Council is bored with Alph. We have bigger problems to solve. We are concerned with nurturing and protecting many thousands, and eventually millions, of new Alphs and the selected young women who will eventually provide mates for them. Whether you agree with the Keisintel laws or not, it has to be done and it is a worthy objective. Alphaville will be one of the key centers—the main nursery, if you like —of our future society. There will be opposition, of course, and perhaps insurrection and world conflict, as you predicted, but it is no bad thing to have an administrator who understands the problems but is still dedicated to the objectives and is determined to achieve them. That is what really matters. As for Alph and Koralin and his other women—our new administrator must find her own humane solution. Above all, she must keep the problem local—very local indeed."

Loron sighed and finished her drink. "Mistress Galinia," she said, "I should like to withdraw my resignation."

Galinia raised her eyebrows in mock surprise. "But it has already been accepted."

"You can withdraw your acceptance, surely?"

"I have never heard so much talk of withdrawal," Galinia observed in mild reproof. "It is highly irregular. I shall have to refer the matter back to Council, and they may wish to see you personally. After all, you are on record as having made some extraordinary remarks about Keisintel policy, and the present generation of Heads of State takes its Keisintel very seriously indeed."

She added: "What future generations may decide is, of course, another matter." And again the swift turn of the head and the quick deliberate wink.

"And how is Alph these days?" Loron asked. Weeks had gone by, and already the new towering shape of Alphaville was reaching upwards to the intense blue sky.

Koralin sat down facing Loron's desk. "Happy and promiscuous as usual, though in a more settled way. He tends to be selective, and this causes some friction and resentment among the women who are rejected. But he likes novelty, so their turn will come."

"Does he ever reject you—his mentor?"

"Sometimes. After all, I am an aging woman."

"Mm—I wonder if he would reject me," Loron mused. "I must try him some time—perhaps when he feels the need for some really outstanding novelty. To be truthful, I am an establishment woman and I prefer the Lesbian syndrome. Now, as to other matters . . ."

She took a long document from the desk. "The first drafts of personnel for Phase 3 will begin to arrive next week—Alpha males and Alpha females. The administrative and scientific organization is already set up and functioning. You, Koralin, will continue to accept full responsibility for Alph, and I'm afraid he must stay in the area allocated to him."

"He prefers to," Koralin said. "On the few occasions when I took him beyond the wall he suffered from an agoraphobic fear—almost terror."

"Well, that makes things easier. You must also use some discretion in allocating his masculine talents among those of the women who fancy that kind of thing. He has to learn responsibility sooner or later."

She paused to consider for a moment, than added: "It's all very irregular, but I suppose non-Keisintel

heterosexual breeding has got to start somewhere sometime. Very well, Koralin—you can have your child. All
I can say is that Alph has a lot to answer for."

"Not really," Koralin murmured. "It was all my fault
—right from the very beginning."

She left Loron's office to return to the young man
who was both son and lover, and whom she had
learned painfully to share with others.

THE END

BALLANTINE BOOKS
TWENTIETH ANNIVERSARY
CLASSIC
SCIENCE FICTION
CELEBRATION

To order by mail, send $1.25 per book plus 10¢ for handling to Dept. CS, Ballantine Books, 36 West 20th Street, New York, N.Y. 10003

1972 SELECTIONS FROM
THE PUBLISHER OF THE BEST
SCIENCE FICTION IN THE WORLD

TIME'S LAST GIFT Philip José Farmer	$.95	**ALPHA 3** Robert Silverberg, editor	$1.25
FIRST PERSON, PECULIAR T. L. Sherred	$.95	**WHEN HARLIE WAS ONE** David Gerrold	$1.25
SEED OF STARS Dan Morgan and John Kippax	$.95	**WOLFWINTER** Thomas Burnett Swann	$1.25
THE TAR-AIYM KRANG Alan Dean Foster	$.95	**ALPH** Charles Eric Maine	$1.25
THE REALITY TRIP AND OTHER IMPLAUSIBILITIES Robert Silverberg	$.95	**THE RESURRECTION OF ROGER DIMENT** Douglas R. Mason	$.95
STARFLIGHT 3000 R. M. Mackelworth	$.95	**TIMETRACKS** Keith Laumer	$.95
THE GOLD AT THE STARBOW'S END Frederik Pohl	$1.25	**SPACE SKIMMER** David Gerrold	$.95
		WITH A FINGER IN MY I David Gerrold	$.95
LIFEBOAT James White	$1.25	**THE BEST SCIENCE FICTION OF THE YEAR** Terry Carr, editor	$1.25

To order by mail, send price of book plus 10¢
for mailing to Dept. CS, Ballantine Books, 36
West 20th Street, New York, N.Y. 10003